The Larkville Legacy

A secret letter…two families changed forever.

Welcome to the small town of Larkville, Texas,
where the Calhoun family has been ranching
for generations.

Meanwhile, in New York, the Patterson family rules
America's highest echelons of society.

Both families are totally unprepared for the news
that they are linked by a shocking secret. For hidden
on the Calhoun ranch is a letter that's been lying
unopened and unread—until now!

Meet the two families in all 8 books
of this brand-new series:

Dear Reader,

Well, here we are at the end of the Larkville continuity. I don't know about you, but I've enjoyed all the stories! I've also enjoyed working with all the authors.

But most of all I've loved Matt, Claire and little Bella. When it comes to writing a story about a man and a woman who are worlds apart, there's nothing like an adorable baby to show them that they are more alike than they think.

For me, as a writer, there is also nothing that comes close to the fun of writing about a brooding billionaire. I love stories that demonstrate that money doesn't buy happiness (because it doesn't!). But stories that prove that real love can save even the most hardened man really knock it out of the park for me.

So settle back, get a cup of cocoa and enjoy Matt and Claire's story. I'm guessing you're going to fall every bit as much in love with little Bella as Matt and Claire did. You'll quickly understand why Claire couldn't leave her with a guy who knew nothing about caring for a baby, and how that one act of kindness drew her into a one-of-a-kind love!

Until next time…

Susan Meier

SUSAN
MEIER

The Billionaire's Baby SOS

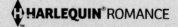

HARLEQUIN®ROMANCE

Recycling programs for this product may not exist in your area.

ISBN-13: 978-0-373-17860-5

THE BILLIONAIRE'S BABY SOS

First North American Publication 2013

Copyright © 2013 by Harlequin Books S.A.

Special thanks and acknowledgment are given to Susan Meier for her contribution to The Larkville Legacy series.

Printed in U.S.A.

Susan Meier spent most of her twenties thinking she was a job-hopper—until she began to write and realized everything that had come before was only research! One of eleven children, with twenty-four nieces and nephews and three kids of her own, Susan has had plenty of real-life experience watching romance blossom in unexpected ways. She lives in western Pennsylvania with her wonderful husband, Mike, three children and two overfed, well-cuddled cats, Sophie and Fluffy. You can visit Susan's website at www.susanmeier.com.

Recent books by Susan Meier

Other titles by this author available in ebook format.

CHAPTER ONE

ALL the ornate boardroom doors that Matt Patterson had faced hadn't been as intimidating as the ordinary brown door before him.

Dysart Adoption Agency.

His chest tightened. His palms began to sweat. His mouth went dry.

Still, he never shirked a responsibility. He opened the door and walked inside.

Wood-paneled walls, an empty reception desk and a soft powder scent greeted him. So did the sound of a baby's laughter. High-pitched and filled with joy, the little-girl giggles and squeals of delight rolled up the hall.

Nine chances out of ten that was his baby.

His baby.

Man, this was going to put a cramp in his love life.

And his traveling.

And his staff.

Good God! The housekeeper, Mrs. McHenry, would have a fit when she discovered they were going to have to add a nursery and a nanny to his already-busy household.

He followed the sound of the giggles to an office at the end of a short hall. Her back to him, a slim woman held a baby in the crook of her arm. Her glossy chestnut-brown hair was swept up in a neat, professional chignon and her red dress rode her curves like an Italian sports car took the turns at Le Mans.

His eyebrows rose. "Somehow I'd always pictured the women who worked at adoption agencies as gray-haired old maids in tacky white blouses."

The baby stopped laughing. The woman at the window spun around.

For the first time Matt could remember, he was speechless.

Huge round brown eyes dominated her face. High cheekbones showcased a pert and proper nose and full, lush lips.

"Can I help you?"

He walked in slowly, his interest piqued. She was exactly the kind of woman he wined and dined, seduced and then left with the gift of a diamond bracelet. But before he could open his mouth to flirt, the baby in her arms squawked. Bella. Oswald and Ginny's daughter. His, because he'd agreed to be godfather to his ex-wife's baby.

Sadness stole over him. This time last week Ginny had called to make dinner plans for when he returned to Boston. Now she and Oswald were gone. He'd never again see Ginny's pretty smile or hear Oswald's goofy laugh. He'd lost the ex-wife he loved and her new husband, who had become a good friend.

Bella screeched again. The woman looked at the baby, then gasped slightly as her gaze jerked back to him. "I'm Claire Kincaid, Bella's caseworker. Are you Matt Patterson?"

Shoving his hands into the pants pockets of his hand-made suit, he ambled into the room. "Yes."

"My God. In four days, Bella's hardly responded to anybody. She doesn't even cry. She eats and sleeps and laughs when I tickle her. But you're the first person she's spoken to."

"Spoken to? Sounded like a squawk to me."

She laughed. "Squawking is how babies talk."

Her pretty brown eyes glittered with humor and his gut tightened. She was *incredibly* beautiful.

"She knows me." He paused. "A bit."

"Because you're a friend of her parents?"

He nodded and took another cautious step toward the woman and Bella. Dark-haired, blue-eyed Bella strained toward him, reaching for him to take her.

Surprised, he jerked back.

Claire Kincaid's smile faded. "She wants you."

"Yes. And I fully intend to care for her but I—" He paused, sucked in a breath. His instincts insisted he should flirt with the beautiful woman. His brain, however, reminded him this wasn't a pleasure trip and he'd better get his head in the game. Somehow or another he'd ended up with a baby and he didn't have a clue what to do with her. "I can't hold her."

"Excuse me?"

He pulled his hands from his pants pockets and raised them in a gesture of total helplessness. "I don't know how."

She took a step toward him. "It's really quite simple."

Her sweet and polite voice matched her nearly perfect face and sent tingly warmth through him. But when she stepped toward him, offering the little girl, he backed up again.

She frowned. "This child is yours."

"And I will take care of her. Next week." He shook his head. "No. That doesn't work for me, either. I have to go to Texas for some family reunion thing—"

The woman holding Bella stopped him with a wave of

her hand. "I don't care if you're the king of the world and you have to hold court. Bella is yours now." She smoothed a hand down the baby's back. "Besides, there's nothing to be afraid of. She's such a sweetie that caring for her will come naturally." She held the baby out to him, and again, Bella strained toward him.

His nervous system rattled like the old-fashioned ticker at the New York Stock Exchange. He'd known for four days that his ex-wife was dead and he was to be Bella's guardian, and he hadn't panicked. He'd handled it the same way he handled everything in his life. He took it one step at a time. But with the baby in front of him, it all suddenly became very real. For the next eighteen years, this child was *his.* He'd have to raise her. Get her through toddler years and preschool, then elementary school, middle school—*teen years.*

"I—" He wanted to take her. He really did. But this was *Ginny and Oswald's* baby. A baby who deserved to be loved and pampered. He hadn't loved or pampered anybody in—well, ever. That's why he'd lost Ginny. He wasn't the pampering, wine and roses, long walks on the beach and talks all night kind of guy. Worse, the people who might be able to help him—his staff—were all out of town.

"Really. I can't take her now. I've been in London for three weeks. When I heard about Bella, I came home early. But I'd dismissed my household staff for the six weeks I was supposed to be away. They're in places like Aruba taking a much-needed break. Even if I called them home, they wouldn't get back before Friday. And I," he said, pressing his hand against his chest, "have absolutely no idea how to care for a baby."

"You don't have nieces or nephews?"

He winced. "No, but even if I did, let's just say I'm not much of a family man."

Though Claire straightened as if she were about to rain down the fire of hell upon him, she protectively rubbed her hand along Bella's back, soothing her. "You agreed to parent a child when you have absolutely no idea of how?"

"I agreed to be a godfather. I didn't realize that also meant I'd be the baby's guardian if something happened to her parents."

"How could you not know that?"

"In some circles *godfather* is a purely honorary term."

Her pretty face softened. "Apparently, your friends took it seriously because you're named Bella's guardian in their wills."

"Yes. But they never told me that and I am just not ready for this."

"You still have to take her."

Disbelief and anger at the injustice of it all reared up in him. Ginny dead. Bella his. It didn't make any sense. Mostly because he wasn't qualified to do this—any of it. He couldn't hold her, let alone change a diaper. And he was the last person who should be assigned to love her.

Bella began to fuss and Claire Kinkaid rubbed her cheek against the baby's, comforting and quieting her.

Inspiration struck like a band of angels singing the *Hallelujah Chorus*. "You're pretty good with kids. What are you doing tonight, Miss Kincaid?"

"It's Claire." She moved her gaze away from his, straightening the collar of Bella's little pink blouse. "And I'm busy."

His eyes narrowed. Busy? She was pretty enough to have a date on a Monday night. If she'd been able to hold his gaze, he might have bought that. "So what you're really saying is that you don't want to help us?"

"We're an adoption agency, not a nanny service." She walked to her desk, pulled out some business cards. "But these are the names and addresses of some well-respected agencies. You could get a stellar nanny from any one of them."

As Claire held out the cards to Matt, Bella blinked slowly. Her long black lashes fell to her cheeks and lifted again. Tears filled her pretty blue eyes, as if she understood she was being shuffled off again.

Sympathy for her swelled in Matt's already tight chest. He had been young, maybe three, when he'd felt odd about his dad—as if he and Cedric Patterson didn't fit together—as if somewhere deep in his subconscious he had always known that he wasn't really Cedric's son. And he didn't belong in the Patterson family. Though Bella was a lot younger, he'd bet that somewhere in her subconscious all of this was being recorded. He could see in her eyes that she might not fully comprehend what was happening, but she was afraid. If nothing else, she hadn't seen her parents in almost a week. She was alone. Frightened.

And though it didn't make sense from a practical standpoint, her emotional well-being suddenly meant more to him than worry over dirty diapers.

He slid his hands into his pants pockets again. "I don't want a nanny. At least not yet. I don't want to leave her with another stranger."

And right now Claire Kincaid was the one person in the world who wasn't a stranger to her.

He caught Claire's gaze and offered the only workable solution. "I'll pay you anything you want to spend the next week with me."

Claire knew the offer was for her nanny services, but her face warmed and her stomach tightened. Matt Patterson might not know how to care for a baby, but he was one good-looking guy. Six foot one if he was an inch, he didn't tower over her, but he was tall enough that even in her heels she had to look up to him. His hair was a shiny light brown, cut short, professional, businesslike. His wicked green eyes smiled when he smiled, and grew stormy cold when he didn't get his way. But happy or stormy they always had a quality of…assessment. As if everything she said or did was of vital importance. And every time he caught her gaze, a lightning bolt of attraction shot through her.

She hadn't had a response to a man in years and her body picked *now?* And *this guy?* A man who'd left his baby with an adoption agency for four days? A man who didn't seem to want to take Bella now? Was she crazy?

"I'm sorry, Mr. Patterson, but as I said before we're an adoption agency. Not a nanny service."

He took a lazy step toward her, sending her pulse into overdrive. The way he looked, everything he did, was just so male. "You're pretty good with her, though."

She took a step back. "Yes. Well, I love children."

"You're better than just somebody who loves children." Studying her face, he frowned. "I'm guessing you got into this business because you were a nanny at some point." His frown deepened and he looked at her even more intently. "Probably when you were in school. Which wasn't too long ago."

Her heart shivered in her chest. He was so close she would only have to lift her hand to touch him, and for some strange reason she itched to raise her hand. Feel his skin. With all his attention focused on her, her body began to thrum.

Stupid hormones! Why pick now to wake up?

She swallowed and took another step back. "I put myself through my first three years at university as a nanny, Mr. Patterson. There is no deep, dark secret about my past."

He smiled. His full lips bowed upward and his green eyes lit with pleasure. "Too bad. Pretty woman like you should have a secret. It makes you mysterious and..." His smile grew. "Interesting."

Her face reddened. Tingles of attraction raced down her spine. Damn, he was gorgeous. And charming. But she knew what happened the last time she got involved with a charming man. She ended up in a bad relationship. A relationship that broke her heart and caused her to stay away from men for five long years.

She forced the business cards for nanny services into his hand. "Dysart Adoption Agency was hired by the attorney for Bella's parents to keep her until you arrived. You have arrived. Our responsibility had ended."

He squeezed his eyes shut. "Fine."

Refusing to fall victim to the helplessness she heard in his voice, she became all business. "Do you have a car seat?"

"My driver picked one up and installed it."

Still holding Bella, she bent and grabbed the diaper bag beside her desk. "Great." She handed it to him. "Those are all the things she's needed for the four days I kept her at my apartment. I imagine there are more things at her parents' house."

"Things?"

"Like a crib. High chair. Baby swing. The things she needs for daily life." Brisk and with purpose, she headed out of the office and up the hall, expecting him to follow her. "I will go with you to your car and help you strap Bella in."

When she reached the office door, he opened it for her

and followed her out, but he didn't say a word. He didn't say a word in the elevator. Standing in the box packed with people, their shoulders brushed. A current of electricity crackled through her.

As inconspicuously as possible, she peeked over at him. With his sloping cheekbones and sexy green eyes, he *was* gorgeous. But she'd met other good-looking men and never felt this. He had power, but power had never been particularly attractive to her. Yet something about him called to her and he wasn't even reacting. Though he'd flirted a bit, it was because he wanted her help. The attraction was clearly one-sided.

She sucked in a quiet breath, glad to be getting away from him. In two minutes, he'd be gone and she wouldn't have to worry she'd say or do something stupid because her hormones insisted she and Matt Patterson should... should... Well, she knew what her hormones wanted.

And that was wrong. Good grief, she'd barely dated since her big mistake her senior year at university when she'd fallen for one of her professors. They'd had a secret affair that started off wonderful and ended when he introduced her to his wife at graduation, humiliating her. Looking back, she realized she should have seen the signs that he was married. He'd pulled her away from her friends, insisted they meet at her place even though he made fun of her condo and never took her out in public. But loneliness after her dad's death had made her vulnerable, needy, and she'd missed the signs.

Which was why, for the past five years, she'd been a woman in control of her emotions. She'd never be so foolish as to fall so fast or be so smitten that she let a man walk all over her. Being overwhelmingly attracted to a guy she didn't know was so out of character it scared her.

The elevator bell dinged. They strode across the building lobby. He pushed on the revolving door, motioning Claire through, into the crisp late-September afternoon. He followed her out into the busy Boston street and paused in front of the black limo parked there. A uniformed man raced to the back door and opened it.

Claire peeked inside. A bar and a television sat across from a curving white leather seat that looked like a plush sofa. But on the sofa sat a car seat.

She quickly passed Bella to Matt Patterson—so quickly he didn't have time to protest and their fingers didn't even accidentally brush. "I'll slide inside, then you hand Bella to me. I will strap her in the car seat, and you can be on your way."

She climbed in. He passed Bella to her. She put the baby into the car seat and secured the straps. As she pulled away, she looked at the baby's pretty face. Blue eyes. Pug nose. Cupid's bow mouth.

Her heart twisted. She'd had this baby with her twenty-four hours a day for four days. Caring for her. Teasing her and playing with her to help her accept her new circumstances. Walking the floor with her as she sobbed all night because she missed her mom and dad. Bella had cried so hard the first night that Claire had cried with her. A baby couldn't understand or deal with death. All she knew was she missed her mom and desperately wanted the comfort of her arms.

Claire swallowed. This poor sweet baby would never see her mom again. Just as Claire hadn't seen her mom after she died.

She pressed her fingers to her mouth. How could she leave this sweet baby with a man who didn't know how to care for her?

She couldn't.

She scooted across the seat and out of the limo. Though

fear trembled through her, she faced Matt Patterson and held out her hand. "Do you have a business card?"

He frowned. "Yes."

"Does it have your home address?"

His eyes narrowed. "Are you planning to do some kind of surprise inspection?"

"I'm going to lock the office, then meet you at your house."

He smiled. Those beautiful green eyes of his lit with so much pleasure, a corresponding pleasure tugged at her stomach. "You're going to help me?"

God help her. "This evening, yes, to get you settled in. Then you're on your own."

CHAPTER TWO

THE rhythm of the car lulled Bella to sleep and she napped through the entire drive home. But when Jimmy, Matt's driver, stopped the limo to punch in the code to open the big black wrought-iron gate for his estate, the baby awoke. She glanced around sleepily. Her little mouth turned down. Her nose wrinkled and she let out with a yowl that went through Matt like an icy wind blows through barren trees.

Pretending not to notice, Jimmy drove up the brown brick driveway. Little Bella's wails filled the back of the limo. She didn't see that the grounds were manicured to perfection. Or that the leaves on the trees had begun to change colors and swatches of red, yellow and orange guided them along the circular driveway to the front of the stately stone mansion.

She didn't care when Matt said, "Shh. Shh. Please stop crying."

She simply continued to wail.

Jimmy appeared at the back door, opened it with a wince. "Quite a set of lungs."

"Indeed." Matt smiled ruefully. "You wouldn't know how to..." He paused, searching for a proper phrase and finally settled on, "Make her stop."

Jimmy backed off. "No, sir. Confirmed bachelor." He

tugged both ends of his bow tie jauntily. "Happily single. Not daddy material."

Remembering what Claire had asked him, he said, "No nieces or nephews?"

"Several but I don't take to them until they're old enough to go the bathroom on their own and get into the casinos in Atlantic City."

He sighed. "An excellent plan." His plan. Until circumstance changed things.

Bella's screams grew louder. He raised his voice to be heard above the sobbing. "So how do we get her into the house?"

Jimmy stepped back again. "Sorry. Not in my job description. In fact, I think I'll go make sure the limo's place in the garage is cleared."

He raced away and Matt scowled. See if the place in the garage is cleared? What a line.

He turned back to the baby. "So…what? You want food? A bottle? Some Scotch?" He knew she didn't want the third, but the terror riding his blood right now had him giddy. *He'd* like a Scotch. But he knew he wasn't getting one. Might not ever get one again until this child turned eighteen.

With Bella wailing beside him, he knew he had a choice. Sit in this limo for God knew how long until the adoption agency woman arrived. Or get Bella out of her car seat and into the house.

A cold wind blew alongside the car. The open door caught it and sent frigid air swirling into the limo. A few drops of rain pelted the limo roof, then the rain started full force.

"Crap."

He reached for the door and slammed it closed. Bella's wails echoed around him.

Jimmy suddenly appeared at the driver door. "Let's get this in the garage!"

"Good idea."

The sound of Bella screaming competed with the drumming of rain on the roof, making a horrendous racket. Matt squeezed his eyes shut, popped them open and turned to Bella. "Come on, kid. You knew me at the adoption agency office." He pointed at his chest. "I'm Mommy's friend."

Her crying only increased when they pulled into the garage. Being indoors seemed to cause the sound to ricochet off the walls and reverberate through him.

He peeked at her face. Little blue eyes watery and sad. Her nose red. Her lips trembling.

He scrubbed his hand across his mouth. He couldn't stand to see her like this. He had to do something!

Noting that Jimmy had disappeared as soon as the limo lurched to a stop, he reached for the buckles of her car seat. Once he had her out of the car seat, he'd carry her into the house and maybe the movement of walking would calm her down?

He found a clasp at her belly that, when opened, allowed him to raise two straps over her head. A buckle by her hip released the bottom strap. When he jiggled the padded half circle around her, he discovered it rose, too.

But with all of her trappings gone, Bella fell forward. He just barely caught her. And when she plopped against him, she wiped her wet face in the lapel of his silk suit.

He groaned.

She clung to him. Using his lapels like a rope ladder, she climbed up and burrowed into his neck.

His heart knotted with confusing emotions. Fear and misery wanted to dominate. He had no idea what to do with this kid. Barely any idea how to get her into the house.

But sympathy snaked through the fear. She was alone. Lost. He knew what it was like to be alone and lost. Except he could also add unwanted. The morning after their legendary fight, Cedric might have retracted his demand that Matt leave the Patterson home, but too many harsh words had been spoken. Up until then, Matt had called Cedric Dad, believed they were blood. But in that awful fight, Cedric had let loose of the big family secret.

Matt and his twin were not Cedric's children. His mother had been married before. She'd left her first husband not knowing she was pregnant, and Cedric had taken her in, raised her children as his own.

It explained why Matt had always felt a distance between himself and Cedric, always felt a nagging sense of not being wanted, not really having a place, not having a home—

He looked at Bella. Orphaned. Alone. With a guy who didn't even know how to get her to stop crying, let alone how to feed her. She could have heard the conversation he'd had with Jimmy about not wanting kids. Not being daddy material. And though he knew that on a logical level she didn't understand a word they'd said, on an emotional level, she'd recorded it all.

Did she feel unwanted?

He pressed his lips together and closed his eyes. His chest shivered with regret. Then he popped his eyes open again, caught Bella beneath the arms and lifted her so they were eye to eye.

"I am sorry for everything that has happened to you in the past few days." His eyes squeezed shut again, as his own grief over losing Ginny and Oswald swamped him.

"Very sorry. I'm going to miss your mama, too. But you're mine now. And that means something."

He wasn't sure what it meant. He *knew*—to use Jimmy's phrasing—that he wasn't daddy material. The best he could do for this kid might be to hire a great nanny or a team of nannies—or maybe find the best nanny on the planet and give her every cent of his money to raise this little girl. But whatever he decided, Matt Patterson didn't abdicate responsibility or say die without a fight.

And as soon as he figured out how to fight, he would fight.

He slid out of the limo, Bella in his arms, and headed for the door into the mansion.

With his resolve in place, he noticed Bella's crying but he reacted to it differently. Something was wrong. He had to fix it.

Unfortunately, he didn't know how. She didn't feel wet. She wasn't generating any god-awful smells. So he steered clear of the diaper area. He asked about food. Mimed feeding himself. She only cried harder. He tried dancing. A couple waltzing twirls caused her to blink in confusion and quit crying for a few seconds, but when he stopped dancing she started crying.

He danced again. Around and around and around the foyer they went. Back to the den where he deposited the diaper bag, took off his jacket and rolled up the sleeves of his white shirt—all while dancing a baby around the sofa.

They danced through the empty kitchen. Up the hall. Around the dining room table. Across the sunroom. Until he felt dizzy and his legs became rubbery.

Where the hell was the adoption agency woman… Claire? Where the hell was Claire?

As if she'd heard him, the gate buzzer sounded. He raced to the com unit and hit the button. "Claire?"

"Yes. It's me."

Her musical voice sent sensation skipping down his spine, bringing her pretty face and sensual body to mind. If she were any other person, if he'd met her any other way, he would date her—

Oh, who was he kidding? He'd sleep with her. But needing her the way he did for Bella, he couldn't even consider sleeping with her. Technically, once she began helping him with the baby, she became an employee.

A smart man didn't hurt a woman in his employ. Especially not one he so desperately needed.

Regret tumbled through him as he pressed the com button. "I'm opening the gate now."

He hit two more buttons and Bella patted his cheeks, as if trying to get his attention.

"What? You want to dance some more?"

She giggled.

What went through Matt's heart was so foreign he couldn't describe it, but it felt like tug of longing crashed into a wall of truth.

He couldn't raise a child. For Pete's sake! He was the Iceman on Wall Street. Unyielding. Intractable. The only thing he knew was severity. Hard truth. He didn't have an ounce of softness in him.

Bella patted his cheek again, squealing with delight, obviously trying to get him to dance some more.

Yearning surged through him, but before he could capture it, it hit that wall of truth again. He was hard, cold. No matter how much he wanted to be the one who showed this child she was loved, that she didn't have to be afraid, he knew he couldn't. His family had taught him that people lied. His ex-wife had shown him that even when he wanted love he didn't know how to accept it.

So how could he show this little girl she was loved? He couldn't.

After parking in front of Matt Patterson's mansion, Claire got out of her little red car and popped her umbrella. Standing in the cold rain, staring at the residence, she suddenly understood what it meant to be a billionaire. Her entire condo building could fit into his house.

She hesitated at the sidewalk. Her heart tumbled in her chest as the reality of what she'd just agreed to hit her. For the first time in five years she was attracted to a man and she'd agreed to spend the evening in his house, helping him care for his baby.

She straightened. This fear was ridiculous. She was an adult. Back when she'd fallen for Ben she'd been a starry-eyed ingenue. She now knew how to control herself.

Plus, this situation was totally different. Matt Patterson wasn't a professor she looked up to. In fact, *she'd* be teaching *him*. There'd be no danger that he'd sweep her off her feet by impressing her with his brilliance. When it came to baby care, Matt Patterson had no brilliance. She'd be fine.

Even before she got to the wood front door with the brass knocker, it opened. Matt stood before her, his hair oddly disheveled, his jacket removed and shirtsleeves rolled up to the elbows. It looked like there might be a thin sheen of sweat on his forehead.

"Come in. Come in," Matt said, all but dumping Bella into her arms after she closed her umbrella and angled it by the door. "I've changed my mind about the nanny. I think we need to get one now."

"Okay." Bella on her arm, Claire slid out of her coat and walked into the foyer. A huge crystal chandelier dominated the space. Her heels clicked on the Italian marble floor. The sound echoed around them.

"I have the cards you gave me in my jacket pocket in the den." He turned and headed down a hall.

Claire followed him.

"But it's all so confusing." He stopped in front of a closed door. "I've never even considered hiring a nanny before." He peeked back at her. "Do I get somebody who's old…old and cuddly…who might want to retire before Bella hits four? Or somebody who's young and sophisticated who might not love her enough. Read her stories. That kind of stuff."

"You're overthinking."

"That's because this is very important to me." He opened the door and led her into a neat-as-a-pin den that could double as an office given that there was an overstuffed sofa and chair in front of a big-screen TV, as well as a heavy oak desk and tall-backed chair on the far side of the room.

He went to the desk and plopped on the chair. But before Claire sat, she sniffed and frowned. "You haven't by any chance changed her diaper in the past hour."

"She wasn't wet."

Her nose wrinkled. "I think she is now. Where's the diaper bag?"

He pointed to the overstuffed sofa where the baby's bag leaned drunkenly against the arm, beside his jacket, which had been tossed haphazardly on the sofa back. "There."

"Okay…so…" She peeked at him. "There wouldn't happen to be a nursery in this house?"

He snorted. "Not hardly."

"Okay." She looked around again, knowing she could make do. "How about a blanket?"

He rose from his chair. "Blanket I can help you with." He frowned. "I think. I know there's a linen closet upstairs somewhere."

"You get a blanket and I'll rummage through the diaper bag for a diaper. Hopefully by the time I'm ready to change her you'll be back with a blanket."

He nodded once and left the room.

When she was sure he was gone, Claire waltzed Bella around the desk once. Rocking the floor with the baby, she'd discovered dancing was the only way to get her to stop crying, but it was also fun. Sort of their point of connection.

"So how's it going with the new daddy so far?"

She screeched and Claire laughed. "You're right. He's green. But think of him as a diamond in the rough."

She danced the baby over to the sofa and poked through the diaper bag until she found a diaper.

She tossed it to the sofa, then danced Bella around again. As the room spun by, she realized how cold and sterile it was and a worry flitted through her. How could a man who lived in such a formal house ever care for a baby? "There's not even an afghan to lay you on."

"Here we are," Matt said, walking into the room. In his hands was a thick blue blanket.

Not wanting to be caught dancing with the baby, she turned her waltz into a step that looked something like she'd been pacing and said, "Lay it on the sofa."

He did as instructed and Claire made short order of Bella's diaper. But even though Matt had meandered away from the spectacle, she caught him peering over a time or two.

A light of hope lit. He might be green and his house might be cold but he was curious. "Want to learn how to do this?"

He pulled back. "No."

"You sure? It's not difficult."

"My hour alone with her was enough to remind me that I don't have the skills to care for her."

"What are you going to do when your nanny takes a day off?"

"Get help from the maid?"

Though that made her laugh, it didn't bode well for sweet Bella. Still, that wasn't her business. The point of her being here this evening was to help him adjust to having a baby, but since he'd mentioned changing his mind about a nanny—thank God—she could also assist him with calling an agency that could provide someone temporary for the night. And Bella would be well cared for.

So she said nothing as she rooted through the few things in the diaper bag until she found a set of clean clothes. One of the four or five sets she'd been alternating with pajamas and washing over the four days she'd kept the baby.

"At some point, you're going to have to go to your exwife's house and get Bella some more clothes. I have several sets of pj's and outfits for daytime in the bag, but it's really only enough for two days. I've had to do laundry twice. Plus, we don't have any of her toys. Things that might make her happy." She glanced around. "You'll also need her high chair and crib and walker and swing."

"I don't even know what half those things are."

She rose from the sofa. "That's okay. That's why I'm here. To help you get set up. What do you say we call your driver and go over to Bella's mom's house and get her high chair and crib, more of her clothes and all of her toys?"

Matt stepped back as a sickening feeling gripped him. Go to Ginny's, when she wasn't there? Knowing she'd never be there again? Knowing he'd pushed her away? Reminding himself of everything he'd lost because he was cold, heartless and the one person who shouldn't be raising her precious baby?

No. Absolutely not.

"I have a better idea. Why don't we just order a new crib and high chair and whatever else she needs?"

Claire laughed. "Why buy new when she already has them?"

Only one of his eyebrows rose.

"Oh, I get it. You're one of those money-is-no-object people."

"And this is bad because...?"

"It's not bad. It's just that it might comfort her to have some of her own things around her."

"If she's been without them for four days, she's probably forgotten them." Guilt warred with pain as he turned to the desk. He knew Claire was right. Having her own things would comfort Bella. But he just couldn't face going to that house. If he had to be strong for Bella, some concession had to be made for him.

"It's been a very long day. This time yesterday, I was in London. Today I'm here...with a baby. Let me get on the phone and make a few calls and buy a high chair and a crib. Tomorrow if she still needs *her* things, I'll make a run for them."

She frowned, as if thinking, and Matt froze. He'd given his best argument. If she disagreed, if she pushed, he had no idea how he'd talk her out of going to Ginny's. Because he couldn't go. He absolutely couldn't go.

Before she could say anything, Bella grabbed Claire's pearls, wrapped them around her chubby fist and stuck her fist into her mouth.

Claire gasped. "Have you given her a bottle lately?"

"I asked, but it didn't stop her crying so I assumed she didn't want it."

She groaned. "You don't *ask*. You show her a bottle." She walked over to the diaper bag, pulled out an empty bottle and kissed Bella's shiny black hair. "Let's go get you something to eat."

Matt raced after her. "I don't have anything for her to eat."

"We're just talking milk here." She stopped, pivoted to face him. "Although we probably should feed her something before we give her a bottle."

"I told you. I don't have—"

She stopped him with a look. "Do you like oatmeal?"

He grimaced. "No."

"Any cooked cereal at all?"

"No."

She frowned and Matt's heart sank. He was going to be a terrible father.

"Pudding?"

He brightened. "Yes! I love the little pudding cups. It's a secret vice."

"A secret vice that's coming in handy." She turned to walk away, but stopped again. "Where is the kitchen?"

He led the way down two halls, and after pushing through double swinging doors, they stood in his restaurant-size stainless-steel kitchen.

"Let me guess. There's a ballroom somewhere in this house."

"Not a ballroom," he said, walking to the first refrigerator. "A party room."

But he stopped and looked around, suddenly seeing what Claire saw. The house was big and beautiful, but it was also cold and intimidating. A child could get lost in here. And feel alone. He did not want Bella to feel alone. He did not want her going through what he went through.

Still, that was the whole point of getting a nanny.

Though he might have to do more remodeling than just a nursery, the nanny would keep Bella busy, happy. As long as he didn't get overwhelmed, he would work all this out.

He pulled open the refrigerator door, reached inside and came out with two little pudding cups. "Chocolate or vanilla?"

"Vanilla for now. Then one of us is going to have to go to a grocery store for real baby food."

"Or we could call."

"Call?"

After getting a spoon from a handy drawer, he directed her to a little table at the far end of the room. "Have a seat."

She sat, settled Bella on her lap and took the pudding cup and spoon from his hands. Bella cooed and reached for it.

As Claire popped the lid, he headed for the desk in the other corner of the kitchen and sat in front of the computer. With a few strokes on the keyboard, he said, "Ah."

She dipped the spoon into Bella's pudding. "Ah?"

"I found our grocer." He made a few clicks on his cell phone and put it to his ear. "This is Matt Patterson. I need to place an order." He waited for his call to be transferred. When someone answered, he said, "This is Matt Patterson. I have a six-month-old baby at my home. I'll need some baby food." He paused, giving the clerk a chance to write down what he'd said. "And some milk." Another pause. "For delivery. Thank you." Then he hung up.

Sliding a spoon of pudding into Bella's eager mouth, Claire said, "You didn't even tell her what kind of baby food you wanted."

"She's paid to know. It's an upscale store."

Bella smacked her lips and grabbed Claire's arm as

if to direct her to give her another bite. Claire laughed. "She's really hungry."

"I see that." He ambled over to the table. "Hey, kid." He crouched so he was eye level with Bella. "You like that?"

She giggled. His first sense of relief in days flowed through him and he smiled. He might not know exactly what to do, but he did have enough money to hire people who did.

He rose. "So diaper is taken care of. Food is handled. I guess it's time we order that crib?"

Bella screeched and slapped her chubby hands against the table. Claire quickly fed her more pudding, then she looked at him. "Yes. We should at least get a crib…and a high chair—oh, and a swing. And a baby monitor for while she's napping. Once we go online and get item numbers—" She made a whirling motion with her hand. "Then you can call whoever it is you call for furniture and baby things and have them delivered."

"Sounds like a plan." A good plan. A wonderful plan. His common sense would carry him through. There was nothing to worry about.

Bella squealed happily, reinforcing his confidence, but a weird sensation tumbled through him. Sort of like he was forgetting something. But he couldn't quite put his finger on it. Still, if it was important he would remember.

He hoped.

CHAPTER THREE

AFTER only five minutes, Bella fell asleep on Claire's arm.

"I think we should go back to the den so we can lay her down while we look for the crib and high chair."

"I can do all this from my phone, if you don't mind looking at this little screen together?"

Their gazes caught. A picture popped into her brain. Them, huddled together, looking at his phone. Her heart would shiver. She'd probably get breathless. All because her hormones had a mind of their own.

"I think the computer in the den is a better idea."

Carrying Bella, she followed him through two ornate rooms, both of which could have been formal living rooms, but at this point she was beginning to see her understanding of houses and architecture was incredibly limited.

Walking to the den, she saw more crystal chandeliers, oriental rugs, hardwood floors and art—everything from paintings to sculptures, vases and blown glass—than she'd seen in her entire lifetime.

She glanced around uneasily. "How do you live in here?"

He opened the door and they walked into the overly neat den. "How do I live where?"

"In a house that's more like a showplace than a house."

"Because of rooms like this," he said, passing the sofa, leading her to the desk with the computer.

She frowned. If he considered this room to be normal, comfortable, he was in worse shape than she'd thought.

He stopped suddenly. "You wanted to lay the baby down."

She pointed at the sofa still holding the blanket from the diaper change. "We just need another blanket to cover her."

He nodded and headed off. She sat on the sofa, Bella sleeping on her lap. Her little pink blouse and baby jeans snuggly fit her healthy body. Her fine, dark hair peaked in little tufts. Her black lashes sat on her cheeks.

In her high school and early college daydreams, Claire had always seen herself as having her own baby by now. And a house. With a wonderful, loving husband who wouldn't work all the time the way her father had. Somebody who'd be home for happy suppers and cozy nights with a storybook to read to their baby.

She snorted a quiet laugh. Yet another reason *not* to be attracted to Matt Patterson. He might be more outgoing than her quiet, quiet father, but he was cut from the same cloth. Work was his sport of choice. Money was the way he kept score. That was probably why he'd so quickly changed his mind about a nanny. Ten minutes in the car with Bella and he'd probably seen how much caring for her would interfere with his life.

Not that she was complaining. As nice as it would be for him to care for Bella himself, a clueless man needed a nanny. Still, it would be wonderful if he did get into the habit of spending a little time with Bella so she wouldn't be as alone as Claire had been as a child.

She swallowed back the lump of sadness and regret that clogged her throat. How she'd longed for a little of her dad's time and attention after her mother died. The lonely days and nights she'd spent flashed to her mind. Nights when she and her businessman father "shared" dinner but didn't speak. Nights when she'd yearned to be tucked in her bed and kissed on the forehead, but never was. Pouring cold cereal for herself for breakfast. Coming home to a quiet house with a maid who didn't like children.

Empathy for Bella rumbled through her. She hoped Matt Patterson wouldn't be a cold, distant dad, but the odds were once he got a nanny he'd slip away. He'd only have contact with the baby when he absolutely needed to. Not because he was bad, but because he didn't know how to be a dad.

He walked into the room, carrying the blanket. "Here you go."

Claire laid Bella on the blanket already on the sofa. When Matt handed the second blanket to her, she opened it enough that it could easily cover the baby.

"There."

"She's okay there?"

"We'll watch her from the desk. But I think she's fine."

"Okay."

With Bella sleeping soundly on the sofa, Matt led Claire to the computer and took the seat in front of it. She stood looking at the screen over his shoulder.

But soon tiredness set in. She'd left the office at four. The drive to Matt's estate had been at least an hour. They'd probably spent another hour changing Bella, feeding her, ordering her food. This on top of a full day's work—and a night of walking the floor with a baby who missed her mom.

She eased her hip to the desk, but Matt's gaze slid over to her rounded bottom. Tingles of awareness floated through her, along with a complication. All this time she'd thought she was just attracted to him.… What if he was attracted to her, too?

He probably wasn't, but just in case, she slid off again.

It wasn't long before her legs pulled at her. She'd been in heels for over ten hours. She eyed his chair longingly, then her gaze caught the sturdy leather arm. Thickly padded and wide, it could accommodate her weight.

Plus, he'd really have to twist and turn to see her butt, her legs, any part of her, because she wouldn't be beside him. She'd be slightly behind him.

Casually, carefully, she eased herself onto the chair's arm. Her feet sighed with relief.

Then her arm brushed his soft silk shirt, she smelled the masculine scent of his shampoo and tingles of electricity shot straight to her middle.

She almost groaned.

He faced her and their gazes connected. Looking into his pretty green eyes made her breathless—but also suddenly curious. He was gorgeous, yet not taken. He had money enough to attract any woman he wanted, yet he lived alone—

Of course, his bossiness probably turned most women off.

So why wasn't it working for her?

They found the product numbers for a crib, high chair, baby monitor and swing. She eased herself from his chair and sat on the sofa, by Bella, as he made a few calls.

Bella began to cry, so she lifted her to her lap. The baby rubbed her tired eyes, clearly feeling the effects of four sleepless nights.

When Matt hung up the phone, Claire said, "So how long until we get the crib?"

"An hour at most."

That surprised her so much she smiled. He was quite the optimist. "Really?"

He rose and headed for the door. "Yes. Give me ten minutes to talk to Jimmy."

"Jimmy?"

"My driver. He'll be the one assembling everything... since I assume cribs and high chairs don't come assembled."

"Probably not."

"Then give me ten minutes to bribe him into helping me."

She laughed, but caught herself, not sure if he'd meant that as a joke. Could stiff and formal Matt Patterson know how to joke?

But Matt wasn't back in ten minutes. In fact, he didn't return to the den for over an hour. Bella had once again fallen asleep in Claire's arms, so Claire put her head back and drifted off.

When Matt popped his head into the den saying, "Delivery truck is here. Jimmy and I will handle this," she bounced up, not sure if she was more embarrassed that she'd fallen asleep or that he'd caught her.

So she didn't immediately go out to the foyer to see what was going on. Instead, she reminded herself that she was only here a few more minutes. They'd put together the crib and lay the baby down—then she'd help him with the call to the nanny service and be gone.

No reason to be embarrassed that she'd fallen asleep. No reason to be bothered about an attraction. In twenty minutes, she'd get in her car, drive off his property and never see him again.

Or Bella.

Her heart constricted at the thought, but she knew that was life. People came and went. Attachments hurt.

She hoisted herself from the sofa and headed out to the hall. When she reached the foyer, it suddenly struck her that she had no idea where he had gone. He'd said he was going with Jimmy to assemble the crib. Which probably meant he was in a bedroom. She glanced around, guessing there could be as many as fifteen bedrooms in this house.

Before she took the thought any further, Matt appeared at the top of the stairway. "Crib's assembled. But we forgot to order sheets."

"Did you notice any flat sheets in the linen closet you found?"

"Yes."

"We'll just use one of those. Tomorrow you can order crib sheets."

"Sounds like a plan."

She carried Bella up the stairs. At the top, Matt pointed down the hall. "This way."

He guided her down two corridors and stopped at a set of double doors. Rich with grain that came through the red mahogany stain, they gleamed at her. He took both knobs, opened the doors and walked inside.

Claire stood on the threshold, her mouth gaping. A huge bed sat on a pedestal in the back of the room, near a bank of windows covered in elegant drapes that looked to be silk. What seemed like half a football field of space sat between the door and the bed, and in that space were a fireplace, white shag area rugs and two club chairs in front of a big-screen TV.

But that was it. The place was so open that gleaming hardwood floors dominated the room.

"This is your nursery?"

"I don't have a nursery, remember? This is my bedroom."

"*Your* bedroom."

"She's going to cry and get up in the middle of the night, isn't she?"

"Yes. But I assumed you'd have the nanny get up with her."

"Not tonight. It feels too much like I'll be abandoning her. That's why I put her crib—" he pointed at an open door to the right "—in there."

"You put her in a closet?"

He snorted a laugh. "No. That's an empty room beside mine. I was going to put an office in there but changed my mind. So it will come in handy tonight. With the door open, she'll be close enough that I'll hear her cry and she won't feel alone."

Gratitude tugged on her heart. She didn't know why this man so easily empathized with Bella's situation, but she was glad he did. Still—

"Do you know what to do when she gets up?"

"Change her diaper and give her a bottle." He headed out of the room. A few minutes later he came back with a flat sheet and walked through the open door into the room beside his. "I watched what you did with the diaper. It didn't seem like rocket science and neither does getting her a bottle."

"I just don't see you walking the floor." She glanced around and took in all the…space. She swore she could fit her condo in the front of his bedroom. "Though there's plenty of floor to walk a baby in here." She glanced around again and finally followed him into the room where the newly assembled crib stood. "My God. Your room is huge. Like a high school gymnasium with better furniture."

"It's adequate." He arranged the sheet on the mattress in the crib.

"It's empty."

"I don't have any need for more than a bed, a few chairs and a TV."

Seeing no point to arguing his personal choices, she laid the baby in the crib. "Whatever. But you still have to consider the hours you'll be spending walking the floor when Bella cries."

"She cries a lot?"

"Nights are the hardest for her."

He combed his fingers through his hair. "I don't want anything to be hard for her. This transition has to be smooth."

"Well, we don't have to make any decisions now. Let's call the nanny service. Maybe there'll be one who won't mind sleeping in the room with the door open?"

"She's going to sleep in the room with the crib?"

"Well, you could give her a suite in another wing, but then she wouldn't hear Bella cry."

"So I have to put a bed in there for her, too?"

"Unless you want to drag one of your chairs over there and make her stay awake all night, watching Bella." She caught his gaze. "And she's probably going to ask you to close the door while she's sleeping."

"Great. That sort of defeats the purpose."

"Not really. Trust me. That close, you'll still hear Bella cry. Plus, you have to make some concession somewhere," she said, leading him out the door.

"I know, but something inside me says I can't leave Bella. I want to be with her tonight. I want her to know she hasn't been abandoned."

Claire's heart swelled again. Her worries that Matt was going to be like her dad, ignoring Bella the way her father had ignored her, lessened a bit. For all his faults, he truly wanted to care for this baby.

They walked out into the hall, but the second the door

to Matt's bedroom closed behind them, they heard a soft cry. By the time they opened the door and returned to the little room with the crib, Bella was sobbing.

As naturally as breathing, Matt reached in and pulled her up into his arms. "Ah, Bella. Don't cry."

Claire's eyebrows rose. He hadn't hesitated. He hadn't deferred to Claire. He'd automatically taken Bella into his arms.

He really wanted to care for this baby.

"You could be very good with her."

"Right," Matt said. His voice rose to be heard above the sobbing. "As you can see, my picking her up really stopped her crying."

"Not yet. But it will. Once she gets accustomed to you." She walked around Matt, noting that his hold on the baby was secure but not a death grip that would frighten Bella. Though his shirt would be permanently wrinkled where Bella leaned against him, he either didn't notice or didn't care. And the baby had her arm on Matt's shoulder, her hand stopped just at his neck. She was beginning to trust him. "You hold her easily, naturally, as if you've done this before."

"I did have her by myself for an hour."

"Hmm." She walked around them again. "You held her the whole time?"

His face reddened a bit. "Yes. Once we got out of the limo I held her."

"And walked to keep her from crying?"

He licked his lips. "Yes. We…walked."

"So maybe you *can* handle her all night on your own."

He glanced down at Bella, who still sobbed in his arms. "I'd rather the baby in my care not cry all night. If a nanny can get her to sleep, then I say we need to bring in those reinforcements."

"Okay. Let's go downstairs and make the call."

They made it as far as the stairway before sobbing Bella leaned out of Matt's arms and toward Claire. Once Claire took her, her crying turned to sniffles, then hiccups, then nothing.

Leading them down the hall to the den, Matt turned. "Amazing. That's at least the second time she's stopped crying for you."

"She's been with me for the four days it took you to return from London."

In the den, he headed for the office section in the back. Claire sat on one of the chairs in front of the desk, Bella on her lap. Bella immediately reached for her pearls.

Leaning in Claire whispered, "Stop that."

The baby giggled. Claire tickled her tummy. "If you want to play, there are more fun things to do than suck on pearls."

Bella squealed.

Claire tickled her belly again. Bella's giggles filled the room.

Matt said, "Okay, dialing now. Everybody might want to put a lid on it so Daddy can hear."

Claire's gaze snapped up. Had he just said Daddy?

"Yes, good evening. This is Matt Patterson. I got custody of a baby today and I'm going to need a nanny."

He leaned back in his chair, obviously listening to what the person at the nanny service was saying, but Claire studied him.

With his perfect hair, sexy green eyes and disarming smile, he didn't look like the kind of guy who would refer to himself as Daddy. Especially not immediately. Ultimately, he'd probably accept the title, but at this point Claire thought for sure he'd fight it.

Something was up with him. Something caused him to see this little girl's plight and respond to it.

But if he got a nanny, a strict one, someone who wouldn't let him help with Bella tonight, someone who wouldn't let him assist with feedings or bath time, he could easily slide out of Bella's life. Grow to depend on the nanny. And then he'd be like her dad. A cold, distant father.

And Bella would have a childhood like Claire's. Lonely.

"You're right."

Matt's gaze snapped to her when she spoke. He put his hand over the receiver. "What?"

"You're right. You can't let her be with the nanny tonight. You have to get up with her. She needs to see you and you need to learn how to care for her."

Matt took his hand off the receiver and answered the person on the phone. "Yes. I'd need someone temporary for a few days while I choose a permanent employee."

She stood up, reached over and pressed the button down to disconnect his call.

"Tomorrow you can get a temporary nanny. Tomorrow we can also ask them to fax some résumés of permanent candidates. Tonight, you need to continue to bond with Bella."

He leaned back in his chair, those sexy eyes holding her gaze. "That had better mean you're staying."

She nodded as the implications of that tumbled through her. "Yes. I'll stay and help."

"And sleep in the room next to my bedroom?"

She lifted her chin. "We're adults. Both of us have the best interest of Bella in mind. Besides, there's a door."

He smiled. "So, I can trust you?"

Her mouth fell open. "Of course you can trust me!"

"Just checking."

But his gaze involuntarily fell to her breasts, then her hips and down to her feet. It was the second time he'd "looked" at her. First the subtle peek at her butt when she sat on the desk. Now a full-scale examination.

She swallowed and turned away, pretending to be pre-occupied with Bella to give herself a second to resurrect her common sense. So he was attracted to her? She was attracted to him and had absolutely no intention of act-ing on it. He was a man too much like her father for her to even consider being interested. And she was a woman who refused to settle for anything less than a loving, won-derful husband.

Neither of them had any worries.

She hoped.

CHAPTER FOUR

CLAIRE faced Matt with a crisp, professional smile. "Since I'm staying the night, I'll need to go home to get some clothes."

Memories of his hour alone with Bella caused him to freeze with fear, not just because of the noise and the feeling of impotence, but because the baby had been so upset. He couldn't stand to see her sob like that again.

He rose. "Are you taking Bella with you?"

"You'll be fine for an hour."

"I think it's too soon to risk it." He didn't want to admit that he couldn't stand to see Bella cry. His feelings ran too deep, connected with too many personal things. Things he didn't care to discuss with a stranger.

So though he didn't lie, he was happy to have the perfect excuse to make sure he wasn't alone with the baby again. "Besides, the car seat is in the limo. We'll all have to go together."

"Fine. I don't care how I get to my house. I just want a pair of jeans and a T-shirt and to get out of these shoes."

She held up her leg to display her red high heels and Matt's gut tightened. He didn't have a shoe fetish, but he did know a good set of legs when he saw them and hers were classic. She was a beautiful woman with great legs who was helping him with his baby. If the odd flutter that took over his stomach any time she was sweet with Bella ever combined with the hot need that exploded through him every time he looked at her, he'd be in big trouble.

Especially since her agreeing to stay for Bella's sake was the kindest, nicest thing he'd ever seen anybody do.

Wincing internally, he told himself not to think like that. Claire was a nice woman and he needed her. He couldn't hurt her. And that's what he did—hurt women. Ginny hadn't hated him after the way he'd destroyed their marriage because he came to the rescue of her second husband, gave him the leg up he needed to become successful. But every other woman he'd dated had. So he didn't date anymore. He had lovers. Women who knew the score.

He texted Jimmy and led Claire through the house to the garage. When he opened the door and motioned her inside, she gasped. "All these cars are yours?"

He barely glanced at the two rows of cars. Everything from a Bentley to a classic GTO. "Yes."

Jimmy suddenly appeared at their right. "And he only lets me drive the limo."

"That's because I'm perfectly capable of driving the other cars." He turned to Claire, motioning to the driver. "This is Jimmy."

"How do, ma'am."

She smiled. "I'm Claire. It's nice to meet you."

Matt said, "We're going to Claire's apartment." He faced Claire again. "Give him the address."

She rattled off the location of her apartment and they got into the limo. She secured Bella in the car seat and just as she had in her first limo ride, Bella fell asleep.

Claire shifted uncomfortably. "So…" Obviously searching for something to say, she finally settled on, "This is a beautiful car."

Matt squelched a sigh. He already liked her. He already

experienced waves of attraction just looking at her. He didn't want them…communicating.

He snorted in derision. "Most limos are beautiful."

"Okay." Clearly getting the message he'd intended to send that he didn't want to make conversation, she turned away, pretending great interest in the scene outside her window.

He looked out the opposite window.

Still, though they rode in silence, his gaze fell to her legs, which were primly crossed at the ankles. With a little flick of a few eye muscles, his gaze could travel from those ankles the whole way past her knees because her skirt had bunched a bit—

Damn it! He wasn't just imagining letting his gaze take a trip up her legs—he had taken the trip!

"She's such an angel."

He jerked his gaze up to Claire's face. She hadn't noticed him gawking at her legs because she stared lovingly at Bella. His gut twisted again. His feelings for Bella were getting tangled up in his feelings for Claire, and strange emotions and yearnings pumped through him. Like desire interwoven with…something. He'd call it contentment but what the hell did contentment have to do with having a baby? She'd been nothing but trouble.…

Except now she was sleeping. Her long black lashes sat on her puffy pink cheeks and her sweet mouth curved upward, filling his heart with the warmth of satisfaction.

He cleared his throat and gruffly said, "Yes, she's an angel," just as Jimmy pulled the limo to a curb and faced them.

"You're not thinking about letting that angel sleep in her seat while you go do whatever it is you have to do here?"

Claire laughed. "Not much of a baby fan, are you?"

"No, ma'am."

But instead of getting angry with the cheeky driver, Claire laughed again. Her pretty brown eyes shone with delight. "At least you're honest."

Matt glanced from Claire to Jimmy and back to Claire again.

Were they flirting?

A surge of jealousy caught him off guard. Since when did he get jealous?

As if only now realizing the limo had stopped, Bella woke and began to cry. Annoyed with himself for being jealous, he reached for the tummy snap, the leg strap and had the round padded thing lifted before Claire could make a move to help him.

"I see you've done this before."

"No thanks to you."

She slid across the seat. "I'm helping you a heck of a lot here. A little appreciation would be nice." Outside the limo, she faced him. "Or maybe we should just go back to your house and I'll get my car so I can come home for real."

Matt's stomach plummeted to his toes. And it wasn't just because he worried about being alone with Bella. He suddenly realized if she left him now, he'd probably never see her again and his heart squeezed.

Good God! He'd known this woman a couple of hours. How could he be jealous, and, worse, afraid of not seeing her again?

He passed Bella to Claire and started across the seat. When he got out of the limo, Claire was halfway up the walk.

Holding the door, Jimmy chuckled. "Better be nice to her unless you want to hear this kid screaming all night."

As Matt entered the building, Claire patiently waited

at the old iron freight elevator of the factory converted to apartments that she called home. She almost wished the thing would have come before he reached her so she could leave him behind. But no. He ambled toward her, looking rich, sophisticated and sexy.

She nervously tried not to notice the exposed brick and pipes that provided a bit of "chic" to the supermodern condos. But every detail popped out at her like objects in a three-dimensional movie. Ben had hated this place. He'd made fun of the pipes, asking if the contractor had run out of money before he could buy materials to cover them. He'd hated the exposed bricks because they were old. He couldn't believe anybody found anything about a factory appropriate to be seen in a residence.

And supersexy, superrich, supersophisticated Matt probably would snub his nose at her condo, too.

She just hoped he had more tact than Ben and wouldn't say his thoughts out loud.

The elevator arrived, she stepped inside and so did Matt.

He didn't say a word as they rose to her floor, but her relief was short-lived when she realized he was probably angry with her for threatening to leave him. Well, she didn't care. Let him stew a bit. She wasn't about to let him talk down to her. After Ben, she'd promised herself she'd never go through that again. And that was one promise she intended to keep.

The old metal doors opened noisily. She stepped out into the hall, once more seeing the brick walls, exposed pipes and hardwood floors. Her resolve strengthened. She loved this building. Loved her home. Let him hate it if he wanted. Let him make fun of it. She didn't care. His feelings meant nothing to her.

Still quiet, Matt followed her down the hall. She held

Bella on one arm as she marched to her door, fishing her keys out of her coat pocket. Before he reached her, she had the door open and was inside.

The exposed brick walls and hardwood floors continued throughout her open-plan apartment. Her kitchen was new, dark cabinets with slim silver handles and stainless-steel appliances. The chic dining area, including a table and trim buffet, flowed into her living room space, which had red sofas facing each other and an overstuffed red print chair with matching ottoman.

"Wow."

She spun to face him. "Wow?"

"Your apartment." He glanced around. "It's so modern." He looked around some more. "I really like it."

Nerves prickled her skin. Her breath whooshed out. She hadn't wanted his opinion to matter, but it had and that bothered her. He might be a nice guy with Bella, but he was also blunt and self-important. Guessing he was only trying to make nice after being rude to her, she grudgingly said, "Thanks."

"I had a similar condo for a while." He smiled as if remembering. "Right after I got my first job. Thought I'd hit the big-time because I started off earning six figures."

She gaped at him. "How does somebody 'start off' earning six figures?"

He strolled around the room. "I went to my interview with two five-year plans. One was for the company interviewing me. The other for their competitor."

She frowned. "So?"

"So, it never hurts to understand what the other guy is probably thinking." He chuckled. "They said I showed initiative."

"It sounds like initiative but I wouldn't know. I've never

been a businessperson, never even thought about wanting to be one."

He strolled over. "You're more of the sensitive type." He took a step that brought them so close she could almost feel the heat from his body. "But we've already discussed this."

"Yes…" She hated the tremble in her voice. He was just so damned good-looking. "We have."

"But we're really not even, you know."

"Even?"

"About what we know about each other. You have a nice condo. You like working with kids. And that's all I know about you."

"I don't exactly know a lot about you."

He chuckled. "You've been through my house." He caught her gaze. "In my bedroom. You know I was divorced but my ex-wife and I stayed close enough that she gave me custody of her child. You've seen my car collection, met my driver. Know that I give my employees long vacations when I travel for business. You know more about my personal life than most women I date."

Her skin flushed. A pulse started low in her belly. So did an unwanted sense of anticipation. It meant something that he was telling her things, or letting her see things about his life through his home. And right now, they stood so close he could kiss her—or she could kiss him, if she wanted.

She swallowed. Suddenly grateful for the protection of the baby on her arm, she said, "Why do you want to know about me?"

"I think you know."

"Because I know so much about you?"

"Because there's something between us." He took another step, forcing her to shift Bella to the left or let the poor baby get squished.

"I don't like unusual things. I don't like unexpected or unpredictable things."

Her breath lodged in her throat. They absolutely could not get any closer.

"So you don't like that you feel something for me?"

"No. I do not."

"Well, thanks."

He chuckled again. "You *should* thank me. You shouldn't want me to be interested. I don't date. I have lovers. I hurt women foolish enough to feel anything for me."

She took a step back, putting plenty of space between them, believing the air had been cleared and they were moving on. "Thanks for the warning." She handed the baby to him, but stopped short of giving her over. "You know, we've been carrying Bella around all day. It might be a good idea to let her roam a bit." She stooped and put the baby on the white shag carpet between the two red sofas. "How's this, sweetie?"

Patting the thick carpet, Bella gurgled up at her.

"Are you sure she'll be okay down there?"

"I've had her on this carpet plenty of times." She rose. "But you're going to make sure she's okay while I'm gone."

"I am?"

"Yes. I'll be five minutes, tops, while I gather a few things. You just have to make sure she doesn't go too far or bump her head or anything like that."

He glanced around. "Okay." He caught her gaze again. "But we're not done talking about this attraction."

"I think we are. You've warned me off enough that I'm not even worried about it."

"Liar."

She snorted a laugh. "What? You think you're so irresistible that—"

He caught her by the waist and hauled her to him. Before she could take her next breath, his lips were on hers. Soft yet demanding, they moved over her mouth until she found herself opening her lips beneath his. He took advantage. His tongue plunged into her mouth.

Desire ripped through her as her body became boneless. Her arms snaked around his neck. He tightened his grip on her waist and the kiss went on…

And on…

Sending sensations careening through her body, making her long for more.

Until Bella screeched.

Claire bounced away like a teenager caught kissing on the front porch by her parents.

Matt sucked in a breath. "Sorry."

With arousal pulsing through her, his apology didn't make sense. She blinked at him. "Sorry?"

"The kiss wasn't supposed to go that far. It was to prove a point." He rubbed his hand across the back of his neck. "I was hoping that…" He winced. "I thought if I kissed you we'd see the attraction was ordinary, and we'd…"

His words acted like water on a campfire. "You hoped I was a really crappy kisser?"

He winced. "Something like that."

She made a sound of disgust. This guy couldn't be any more infuriating if he tried. How could she be so attracted to him? "I'm going to get my things."

She turned to walk away but he caught her arm.

"I am sorry. But everything's getting confused. I'm trying to tell you that I'm not a family man, not the settling-down kind. Being with Bella is making me look like I might be…or maybe I should be. But I'm not."

Her face grew tight with an emotion so strong yet so foreign she couldn't even describe it. She'd never had a man tell her he was attracted to her as he tried to talk himself out of it. She wasn't sure if she was humiliated or infuriated.

"I get it."

"I don't think you do. The family reunion I'm going to in Texas is a joke. My family is riddled with secrets and lies.... No, I take that back. My family was *built on* secrets and lies. I became calloused to survive and I have survived. I've thrived. You're not like the sophisticates I date. And if you get involved with me, you will end up hurt."

She straightened her shoulders. What did he think she was? A lovesick schoolgirl? Ben had cured her of that. "Got it." She turned to go, but pivoted around again. "And just for the record, you might be a great kisser, but I'd already realized you're not a great catch. You're blunt. You're rude. You're absolutely positive you're always right. Well, this is one time you aren't. I wouldn't date you on a lost bet. You're everything I avoid in a man. I learned that lesson young because my dad was exactly like you. Cool, efficient. Silent most of the time. And if that isn't enough, I had a boyfriend who used me. So don't think I'm helping you because of your supposed charm. I'm helping you for Bella's sake." She took the two steps that separated them and got in his face. "You...are...perfectly... safe...with...me."

With that she walked away and Matt scrubbed his hand across his mouth. Well, that hadn't gone well. He'd had the best of intentions when he'd warned her off. She was a nice girl and she was attracted to him. And he didn't want her to get hurt. Yet his good intention of sparing her feelings had actually ended up making her mad.

He blew his breath out on a sigh and walked over to

Bella. Stooping down so he was on her level, he leaned in and whispered, "She'd probably kill me if I told her that she was even sexier when she yelled at me."

Bella squawked. He picked her up and rose with her. "What? You don't like the adults not paying attention to you?"

She laughed and patted his face and he smiled at her. But his smile quickly faded. Claire was right. He really was getting accustomed to this kid. He hadn't thought twice about picking her up. Didn't mind holding her now.

So maybe this was going to work? Maybe he could be a good dad?

Claire came out of her bedroom carrying a small duffel bag. Matt hardly noticed it. Seeing her hair down around her shoulders, fat curls that bounced when she walked and her plain top that hugged her curves before it stopped at the waistband of her low-riding jeans caused his mouth to water. Memories of their kiss thundered through him. Had he been a bit hasty in warning her off?

No. He'd been fair. He needed help with Bella and Claire was obviously providing it. Because she cared about Bella—not him. Not even his money. Good Lord, she hadn't even hinted about compensation.

He frowned. It was the first time since he'd gotten rich that somebody had just helped him.

Grabbing a bright red leather jacket, she said, "Let's go," and headed for the door.

He scurried after her. His gaze automatically fell to her bottom showcased in low-cut jeans, and inwardly he groaned. But he hadn't made a mistake in warning her off. He needed her. Her reward for helping him would be that he wouldn't hurt her.

When they reached the limo, Jimmy jauntily opened

the door for Claire and she smiled at him, said, "Thanks," a little breathlessly, and Matt's blood pressure rose.

He handed Bella into the limo and Claire strapped her in the car seat as he settled on the seat across from her. A bit miffed that she'd sort of flirted with Jimmy again, he decided not to talk to her.

But after ten minutes of silence in the car, he realized *she* wasn't talking to *him*.

His heart squeezed. But he ran his hand down his face. This was ridiculous. They'd both outlined very good reasons why they should stay away from each other. Hadn't his heart and hormones been paying attention?

Claire tapped on the round padded thing that kept Bella securely in the car seat. "Hey, sweet girl."

The baby gurgled a laugh.

"We should have remembered to bring something for her to play with."

He grudgingly peeked over. "Like what?"

"She came with a bear and I bought her two rattles and a chew toy. They're in her diaper bag."

"We'll give them to her when we get back."

She smiled. "Okay."

He simmered. She seemed very happy. Relaxed. Almost as if their kiss hadn't happened. Or maybe she was happy that they'd cleared the air between them?

Well, fine. He was happy, too. God knew he had a million other things to think about, worry about, stress over, if he wanted to be stressed.

His already unhappy family had been increased by four half siblings. The children his real father had had with the woman he married after Matt's mother had returned to New York. And he had to meet those people in nine short days. For his sisters' sake, he'd promised to be nice.

If he wanted to obsess over anything, he should be

figuring how he intended to keep his promise to Ellie, Charlotte and Alex. Having all recently settled down— Charlotte with a baby even—they were now all about family and wanted him to be part of that, too. He shouldn't be worried that the current woman in his company was the first woman in a long time to not only reject him, but also to stand up to him.

Great. Now he was thinking about her again.

Maybe the mistake was agreeing to let her spend the night…

In the little room next to his bedroom…

This was going to be peachy.

CHAPTER FIVE

By the time they arrived at the mansion, it was dark. Jimmy drove the limo into the garage, and as soon as it stopped, Claire reached for the buckles and snaps to free Bella.

She carried Bella to the door as if she'd been to his house a million times, walked through and headed to the kitchen.

Matt stayed on her heels, not exactly sure what he was supposed to do. She took a bottle from the diaper bag, rinsed it, filled it with milk and walked out of the kitchen up the hall, toward the curved stairway in the foyer. "First a bath, then some milk, then it's into bed with you, Missy."

"It's only eight."

Walking up the stairs, she faced Matt. "She's a baby. Babies go to bed early."

"Did you ever stop to think that if you kept her up until ten, she'd sleep through the night?"

"You're wishful thinking."

She walked into his bedroom and stopped at the three side-by-side doors along the left wall. "Which door?"

"For?"

"The bathroom. She needs a bath, remember?"

"Middle one."

She opened the door onto his master bath, and though

she started to step in confidently, her foot faltered. "Good God."

He ambled up behind her. "What?"

He didn't think it was the Italian marble floor that stopped her. The double sinks were special, especially since there was a waterfall that ran down the brown, gray and white stone tiles behind them. But they didn't usually earn a gasp. The huge shower was cool. He loved the showerhead that felt like rain and the jets that shot water out of any side or corner of the shower he wanted, but most people didn't notice the wonders of the shower until they were in it.

So, she had to be gaping at the old-fashioned claw-foot tub.

Sitting on a one-foot marble rise with a solid-gold faucet, beneath a skylight that probably right now had a great view of the stars, the tub could be a showstopper.

"You bathe in that?"

"Well, I don't want to walk around smelling like a wildebeest."

"I guess you feel like Napoleon when you're sitting in that thing."

"Actually, I fancy myself more like Julius Caesar." Happy to finally be in control again, he said, "I light a cigar, lay my arms along the rims, put my head back and look at the stars."

She cautiously walked over to the tub. Her head craned back until she saw the skylight. "Ah."

He snuck up behind her, whispered in her ear. "Pretty nifty, isn't it?"

"This bathroom is bigger than my entire apartment."

"Want to see the rain shower?"

She faced him, swallowing. "I'd just like to see a normal tub where I could bathe a baby."

"She'd probably fit in the bowl sinks."

"In front of the waterfall?" She glanced around again. "Sheesh. Man. Do you really need all this stuff?"

"It's my reward."

"Well, you must have worked your butt off to feel you deserved all this."

"I did. And it makes me happy."

It really did. Being in this room reminded him that this was what he'd been working for his whole life. The freedom to live his life as he wanted. His mom had lied to him about Cedric being his father. He'd never felt he fit into his own family. He had even become distant from his sisters, who didn't care about real dads and pretend dads and bloodlines or lies. But he fit here. He was happy here. And some five-foot-seven slip of a woman wasn't going to make him "think" he wanted something else out of life. Especially not after only a few hours.

Besides, she was here to help him with the baby, to show him the ropes. He didn't want to waste this opportunity.

He strolled over to the first sink where she ran water while she pulled out a diaper and one-piece sleeper from the diaper bag one-handed.

"Here. Let me hold her."

Not meeting his gaze, she handed the baby to him. "Thanks." When the baby was securely on his arm, she said, "Is the linen closet around here?"

"What do you need?"

"Towels. A washcloth."

He walked over to the corner, pressed a button and the wall opened. He pulled out two fluffy white towels and a washcloth. "Here you are."

While he was gone, she'd removed a pink bottle, a

little yellow bottle and a taller white container from the diaper bag.

"What are those?"

Taking the baby from him again, she said, "Lotions and powder. Baby wash. Nothing special."

He frowned. Had that been a quaver in her voice?

"Are you okay?"

Removing Bella's one-piece outfit, she said, "I'm fine."

But not chatty. He knew he'd discouraged conversation in the limo, but she'd seemed fine, bossy even, until… He glanced around. Until they'd started talking about his tub? This bathroom?

Maybe he'd flaunted his wealth a bit too much. Or maybe his casual comments had seemed to her as if he was rubbing her nose in his success.

"Look, I'm sorry if I came across as an idiot talking about my tub. I didn't mean to upset you."

"I'm not upset."

"Your voice says you are."

She sighed and sat naked Bella in the sink she'd filled with water. "Okay. I'm not upset as much as reminded of some things I'd rather not think about."

"Ah. The bad boyfriend."

"No, the distant dad."

"Your distant dad had a big claw-foot tub?"

"Among other things." She rinsed water along Bella's tummy, and made the baby laugh. "My father was a successful businessman." She slanted him a look. "Not anywhere near your caliber, but he did okay." She shook her head. "He lived for the deal."

Yet another reminder of why he shouldn't get involved with women. He lived for the deal, too. And Claire's current sadness was the reminder of the fallout of that kind of life. "I bet that thrilled your mother."

"My mother died when I was six."

"Oh." That news shifted through him oddly. He could picture her. A little girl with big sad brown eyes and long brown ponytails, left alone by a dad who didn't know how to care for her.

His stomach knotted and he understood why she was so sympathetic to Bella. Right then and there, he strengthened his commitment to be the best father he could for his little girl, even as his chest tightened with sorrow for Claire's loss. "I'm sorry."

She poured one of the gels onto the washcloth, worked it into suds and leisurely ran the cloth over Bella's soft skin. "It's certainly not your fault."

"I was apologizing for bringing up unhappy memories."

"It's okay."

It really wasn't. Not just for Claire, but for him. He'd spent most of his adult life upset over his mother taking him away from his real father and saddling him with a stepfather who didn't want him, and then angry that his biological dad never tried to find him, to meet him—to anything.

But after hearing of Claire's losses he felt like a heel.

He pointed toward the bedroom. "I'm going to go check on the crib, make sure that sheet is okay."

She nodded. "Okay."

Inside the bedroom, out of Claire's sight, he ran his hand down his face. He got it. Lots of people had lives worse than his. But that didn't diminish the fact that he had some problems. Not only did he have to meet four half siblings, but the twin and half sisters he'd been raised with would be in Texas, too. He had to meet his new siblings and deal with the old ones, when he was turned inside out about raising a baby because he'd lost Ginny. The one person who'd always loved him. Any other ex-wife would have been happy to be rid of him, but she'd kept him as a friend, made sure he had a part in her life even after she remarried. There was no one like Ginny who'd understood the real Matt Patterson and still liked him. True, she couldn't be married to him but they had been friends. Good friends.

But now she was gone. And for the first time since he'd met Ginny, he was alone in the world.

Truly alone.

Claire lifted Bella out of the sink and rolled her in the thick fluffy white towel. She tickled her tummy and played with her a bit, but inside she was dying. The loneliness she'd felt after her mom's death rolled over her as if it were yesterday, not decades ago. And she wished… well, she wished Matt would have comforted her. After that kiss, it was clear they both were attracted. Neither one could deny it. But he couldn't find it in his heart to stay in the room and comfort her…or even really talk about her life.

Still, that was her luck with men. Her friends found good men, strong men, who knew how to love, how to comfort. She always seemed to be attracted to the self-absorbed guys.

Like Ben. He hadn't really loved her. But she'd thought he had. And she'd loved his company. She loved having somebody to spend time with, somebody to think about the future with. But when he'd introduced her to his wife at her graduation—the day she'd believed he would propose to her—her whole world had fallen apart. Instead of proposing, he'd broken up with her. And not by saying, "I'm sorry. It didn't work out." No. He introduced her to his wife. A not-so-subtle way of saying, "Now, that you're leaving the university, I have no need of you."

Discovering he was married and realizing her loneliness had driven her to a bad relationship didn't ease the pain of being alone after he was gone. Her bed wasn't just empty; her life was empty. She had a fancy condo, new car and a degree, but her life was empty.

And that was what she saw when she really looked around this house—Matt's house. Everything was perfect, beautiful, but untouched.

She rolled Bella into clean pajamas, telling herself Matt Patterson's "untouched" house wasn't any of her business. But she knew he was lonely, and his beliefs about relationships would keep him lonely. At least she was up front about her loneliness. At least she was trying to find real love in her life....

She snorted a laugh that made Bella giggle. Trying to find love? She hadn't been attracted to a guy since Ben. Five years. And the first guy she's attracted to is cold and unfeeling.

Yeah. She was brilliant at picking partners. Brilliant at working to cure her loneliness.

Still, he'd warned her he wasn't the kind of guy who settled down or wanted relationships. She would be a good soldier and believe him.

She lifted clean and dressed Bella from the counter and nuzzled her neck. Matt Patterson might be a crappy choice for a boyfriend, but like it or not he had to be a dad. For Bella's sake, she'd do whatever she could tonight to help him learn how to love this baby.

She carried Bella out of the bathroom and walked her into the room beside Matt's bedroom to find Jimmy helping Matt put together a single bed.

"What's this?"

"Well, I certainly didn't want you sleeping on the floor."

She hadn't forgotten she was sleeping in the room next to Matt's, but watching them put together a bed made it all very real.

"I called Jimmy and we brought this bed from storage."

Jimmy inclined his head in greeting. "Brought your duffel bag up, too."

She smiled. Jimmy was a funny, nice guy who didn't put up with any crap from his boss, who seemed to have a knack for making her laugh. "Thanks."

As they put the bed together, she carried Bella to one of the club chairs in front of the TV in Matt's room and fed her a bottle.

When the bed was together, Jimmy left. Bella finished the last of her milk, her eyes drooping. Matt left the room for a minute and returned with clean linens.

Realizing they were for the bed she'd be using, Claire rose from her chair with sleeping Bella. "I'll get those."

"No. I'm fine." He dumped the sheets on the single bed. "You take care of Bella."

"She's asleep." Claire laid her in her crib, wondering how the heck this rich guy who wasn't quite sure where to find a blanket knew so much about sheets. Not only was he making her bed now, but he'd put the sheet on the mattress in Bella's crib. "And my work with her is done. So I can get those."

"How about if we both do it?"

She walked over to the bed as Matt opened the fitted sheet, billowing it across the bed so she could catch her end and hook the corners over the mattress.

When it was on, Matt did the same thing with the flat sheet.

Uncomfortable with the silence between them, Claire said, "We really are running out of clothes for Bella."

"We can buy new."

"I know but she probably has tons of her own things. Wouldn't it be nice to have some of the pretty things her mom picked out for her?"

Matt's heart somersaulted. He knew Claire's intentions were good, but every time he thought about Ginny his sadness got worse.

"Especially for that trip to Texas you're taking. She's going to be in a new environment again. It would be better for her to have some toys and her own clothes. Comfort things."

Matt sniffed. "Comfort things?" He shook his head. "I'm the one who needs the comfort things. The whole trip-to-Texas family-reunion thing is going to be hell."

"Hell?"

He stuffed a pillow in a pillowcase. "I haven't really been involved in my family for a decade and this 'reunion' is all about meeting half siblings I didn't even know I had."

"You have stepsiblings?"

"*Half* siblings. It's a long story."

She glanced at sleeping Bella. "We have time."

"My family doesn't matter. I have Bella now. She's my family. My life is busy. I have too much work to do to get involved with those people. In fact, the smart thing to do would be just not go to Texas. That way I won't have to worry about Bella adjusting to more new people. We'll stay here with her nanny, adjusting to the world she's going to stay in, not visiting a bunch of people she'll never see again."

Shocked, Claire gaped at him. "Just like that, you're giving up family?"

"My family isn't the white picket fence, nice guys who sit around a Thanksgiving table counting our blessings. We keep secrets. We hide things. I'd rather be alone than be with them."

He sucked in a breath. "Bed is made. Bella is sleeping. If there's nothing else for me to do, I'd like to go downstairs to make some west coast calls."

"Sure."

He headed for the door, but stopped. "Make yourself at home. Shower if you want. Get yourself some cocoa or a snack in the kitchen."

She nodded.

He walked out of the room, closing the door behind him.

She glanced at Bella, sleeping soundly in the crib, and lifted her duffel bag from the floor beside the bed. She rummaged around until she found pajamas and her cosmetics case and took those into the big bathroom.

After pulling out her body wash, shampoo and other shower essentials, she stripped and walked to the big shower. She smiled. Good grief. Such luxury! She'd given up being pampered almost a decade ago, but suddenly a shower with sixteen body jets seemed like a lot of fun.

But when she was in the cube, being pelleted with warm water, the echo of the spray in the shower brought her up short. When she stepped out and dried herself in the ultrasoft towel, the sound of nothing—not another person, not a car on the street, not a TV or radio or CD player…nothing—assaulted her.

This was how he lived.

This man who rejected family, who said he didn't need people, who said he loved his life, lived with servants and silence.

CHAPTER SIX

DRESSED in her pajamas and robe, Claire took Matt up on his offer and made herself a cup of cocoa in the cool, impersonal stainless-steel kitchen. Her every movement echoed around her in the quiet, underscoring the emptiness of the house.

A huge ball of empathy for Matt lodged in her tummy and the temptation was strong to go in search of him—if only to provide company. She suspected he was in the den, but with the size of his home, she also knew he could have a totally different office in another wing somewhere and her trip would be wasted.

Still, she stopped at the bottom of the stairs in the foyer. Her intimate knowledge of the pain of loneliness wouldn't allow her to let anyone else suffer. But he didn't want help and she didn't want him to think she was interested in him romantically. They might have kissed and both enjoyed it, but they'd agreed they wouldn't pursue their attraction. Plus, as he'd said, he had Bella to be his family. He didn't need anyone else. What business was it of hers to think that wasn't enough? Why should she care that he had family he didn't wish to see?

She shouldn't.

The wise course would be to simply do what she was

here to do—help him care for Bella tonight—and leave him tomorrow.

She climbed the steps, walked through his bedroom to the single bed near the crib and removed her e-reader from her duffel. Curled under the covers, she read for an hour, so engrossed in her book she didn't even feel time passing and suddenly the bedroom door opened.

Matt walked in. "Hey."

She set down her e-reader. He looked tired and sad. Longing to make him happy rose up in her. But they'd agreed not to get any further involved than they had to be for Bella.

So she said, "Did you get your calls made?"

"Yes." He rolled his shoulders as if exhausted. "Bella still sleeping?"

"Soundly." She glanced at the crib and smiled. At least something was going right. "In the four days I had her, she usually woke around ten. Since she slept past that, I think she's happy with the new crib."

He breathed a sigh of relief. "That's good."

Claire narrowed her eyes. If he'd been worried that the baby wouldn't like the new crib, why had he insisted they buy one? They could have easily gone to his ex-wife's home and retrieved Bella's old one. So why had he argued?

He motioned toward his room. "I'll just take a few minutes in the bathroom—brush my teeth and stuff—and I'll check on you guys again."

Once again telling herself that things about him and his life were none of her business, she simply said, "We're fine. You don't need to check on us."

He nodded and left the room. But in the bathroom, he leaned against the sink. He could smell her. The scent of flowers saturated the entire room. It could have been her soap or her shampoo. It didn't matter. Whatever it was, it swirled through his nostrils, tickled his senses and awoke needs he didn't want to feel for a sweet woman like Claire.

He shook his head. Could she have picked more prim and proper pajamas? Pink like cotton candy, the pants went the whole way to her ankles and the top buttoned at her throat.

He might have thought she'd dressed so primly to make a point, but something in his gut told him pajamas like those were what she regularly wore to bed. She wouldn't try to entice a man.

He frowned. She didn't have to. For some reason or another her proper clothes were sexier to him than the slinky red and black cocktail dresses worn by women with long nails and big ideas for how to pass the time until dawn.

With Claire he'd be the one doing the seducing....

Groaning, he told himself to stop thinking about her. He stripped, showered and brushed his teeth in record time. He walked to the closet at the back of the room and rummaged until he found an old pair of pajama bottoms, a gift from Charlotte, and slid into them, along with a robe.

If she wanted to be proper, he would be proper.

He strode through his bedroom, to make one more check on them, but Claire only said, "Good night," and rolled over onto her side.

Okay. Fine. She wanted to go to sleep; he would go to sleep. It was late. After eleven. He didn't have a problem with that.

Still, he tiptoed toward the crib for one final look at sleeping Bella. Her lashes rested on her plump rosy cheeks. Her lips were bowed in a smile. He wondered if she was dreaming about her parents and his heart skipped a beat. Even with all the trauma in his life, he couldn't imagine what she was going through. He prayed he would be a good dad to this poor sweet child.

Then he left the room, shrugged out of his robe and climbed into bed—his bed on a pedestal.

Unable to relax, he sighed, plumped the pillow. He'd slept in this exact bed for years, lots of years, and suddenly tonight it seemed wrong for him to be in this big bed, like some king.

He wasn't a king. He was an outcast. An outcast who'd used his wits and education to best every competitor who came his way.

He'd won.

Yet, tonight it didn't feel like he'd won. Caring for Bella made him feel ill-equipped and vulnerable. And merely considering breaking his promise to his sisters, Charlotte especially—the only person in his family he still spoke to—and not meeting the family he didn't want to meet, had also put him on edge.

Which was probably why he'd let some things slip to Claire when she'd asked about his family. He'd never wanted to talk about them before. But suddenly, with her, it was so easy to spill his guts. He blamed it on nervousness over the upcoming trip and once again considered not going. He didn't want to know these people. He was fine on his own.

But what about his promise? Was he bound by a promise he'd made to his sisters in a moment of weakness?

He flounced onto his side, annoyed with the direction of his thoughts. Especially when he began to consider all the possibilities for fights and backbiting when the Calhoun and Patterson clans got together. Technically, he was the oldest of the Calhoun children, but his "brother" Holt ran the family ranch, watched over the family holdings and "distributed" profits. With no will specifically naming Holt leader of the pack, Matt could come in and assert his rights. After all, who better to manage a family's fortune than a man who'd made one for himself?

He didn't want to think about how they probably planned to intimidate him into falling in line with Holt's wishes. He'd rather think about Claire and her pretty pink pajamas not trying to seduce him but making him crazy with wanting her.

It was no wonder he'd kissed her.

Remembering the feeling of her soft mouth against his, the mating of their tongues, the intense heat that whooshed through him, he almost groaned. But she was in a bed only a wall away and, if he groaned, she might hear him.

And she would ask what was wrong because she was considerate like that, and God only knew what he'd say this time.

He pulled the covers over his head. What the hell was wrong with him? He never wanted to talk to anybody! Why did he suddenly want to talk to her?

He was letting her get too close. That was what was wrong. She was here to help him with the baby and he was out of his element, so in his vulnerability he was making mistakes. But no more. He would learn what he needed to know as quickly as he could so this unwanted vulnerability would go!

Bella's crying woke Claire at around three. She'd slept an hour later than usual, which was good, but she hadn't slept through the night.

Realizing all this was new to Matt and that some of it had clearly overwhelmed him, she rolled out of bed and sped to the crib.

"Shh. Shh." She reached in and pulled out Bella. "I've got you! Give me two minutes to change your diaper and we'll race to the kitchen to get your bottle."

"I'll get a bottle."

Matt's voice from behind almost made Claire jump out of her skin. She whispered, "You scared me!"

Matt headed for the door. "No need to whisper. With her lungs, Bella could have the whole household up by now...if anybody was here."

She went to reply, but Matt opened the door and left before she could. No matter. She took the baby to the bathroom, found a diaper and had her changed before Matt returned with the fresh bottle of milk.

As he walked over to her, she sat on edge of her bed. But instead of handing the bottle to her, he took the baby. "We need a rocker in here."

Shocked that he'd taken Bella and had arranged her on his arm to feed her, she gaped at him. "What are you doing?"

"Feeding her."

"I can do it. You go back to bed."

"I need to learn how to do this and I am."

Respect for him rose up in her. Her father had passed everything to the various maids they'd had over the years. But Matt really wanted to care for Bella. She patted the bed beside her. "You'll get a rocker tomorrow. Until then, you can't stand to feed her." She grimaced. "Well, you could. But it takes a few minutes for her to eat, so you're better off sitting."

He grunted, brought Bella to her bed and sat on the spot Claire had patted.

Bella gulped greedily and Claire laughed. "Are we a little piggy tonight?"

Bella grinned around the bottle's nipple.

Matt slanted her a look. "Are we allowed to talk to her?"

"Sure. It's like dinner conversation. It helps you to bond." She paused, smiled at him. "Try it."

He quickly glanced away. "I don't know what to say."

"Say anything." She paused. "Why not tell her about the new family she's about to meet in Texas?"

He rose. "She's getting done really quickly. We don't have time to talk."

Disappointment skittered through her. It wasn't good for Bella to have him running hot and cold. And when it came to family he was definitely hot and cold. So she moved them off the topic of the Texas reunion and said, "You should probably burp her."

He spun to face her. "Burp her?"

His incredulous question made her laugh. "If you don't burp her the gas will wake her up."

"The first thirteen years of my life I heard nothing but don't burp…now you want me to get her to burp."

"Your mom probably never said don't burp. She probably said don't burp in public."

He snorted a half laugh. "All right. Whatever. How do I burp her?"

She hoisted herself off the bed and walked over to him. Lifting Bella from his arms, she said, "You have to put her over your shoulder." She arranged the baby on his shoulder and he quickly put one hand beneath her bottom and one hand on her back. Their fingers brushed. Electricity skipped up her arm, reminding her of their kiss, but she ignored it.

"There. See?" She took a step back and quickly turned to walk back to the bed, far too tempted to check his face to see if he'd felt the zing, too. "Now, all you have to do is pat her back until she burps."

He patted and Bella burped loudly. "Well, that's interesting."

"That's actually great. Now, give her the bottle again."

Bella finished her bottle, burped again, then fell asleep. Matt whispered, "So do I put her in bed?"

"Yes, but expect to get up again soon. She's never slept this much before."

Sympathy for Bella flashed across his face, and Claire looked away. He was far too handsome and she was far too attracted to him to let all the sympathy and empathy she knew he felt sway her. Combining his good looks and her attraction with appreciation for his love for Bella, it wouldn't be long before she found herself genuinely liking him—and they'd already decided they weren't going there.

With Bella in her crib, Matt returned to his room and Claire crawled under the covers on her bed again. She nearly got out her e-reader, expecting Bella to awaken soon and not wanting to fall asleep only to have to wake up again. But she drifted off to sleep and didn't have another thought until the sound of Bella crying caused her to bounce up. Faint light peeked in at the meeting of the drapes. It had to be at least seven!

This time, she lifted Bella from her crib, took her into the bathroom and got her cleaned up for the day without waking Matt. She put her fingers over her lips to silence giggling Bella as they sneaked through Matt's room to the bedroom door.

She was just about done feeding Bella some of the cereal that had been delivered the night before when Matt sleepily entered the kitchen.

"I told you I want to help. You should have gotten me up for this...and when she got up again last night."

He wore the navy blue pajamas he'd worn the night before. A big navy velour robe hung loosely on his shoulders. Untied, the belt dangled to the floor and followed behind him like a thin train.

Still, with his hair sticking out in all directions and his eyes drooping sleepily, he was incredibly sexy. Sort of messed up like a guy who'd spent the morning making love. And much more approachable than the guy in the white shirt and handmade suit.

Knowing her brain had gone in a bad, bad direction, she turned her attention away from him and onto the baby as she answered his question.

"That's just it. Bella didn't get up last night. After her three o'clock feeding she slept until now."

Halfway to the counter, he stopped, faced her. "She did?"

"Yes!" She lifted Bella off her lap and nuzzled noses with her. "Our girl had a good night's sleep. In the four days I had her she barely slept four hours. With you, she's sleeping."

Matt's heart about stopped. "That's good?"

"That's excellent!"

He swallowed the lump of emotion that formed in his throat. He might not be brilliant at parenting. Hell, he might not be ready to parent, but it seemed Bella trusted him. That gave him such an emotional high he could have happily kissed Claire, but everything that had happened between them the day before came tumbling back and his chest tightened.

He didn't want to get involved with her. Worse, he didn't want her to know how tied in knots she had him. So he headed for the counter and pulled out the coffee and filters.

"You still should have woken me when she got up."

"There was no need."

Pouring grounds into the filter, he said, "She's my responsibility and I take my responsibilities seriously."

To his complete surprise, she sniffed a laugh. "No kidding. A guy doesn't get to be where you are by shirking his responsibilities." She paused, glanced around. "Unless you inherited your money."

"No. I didn't."

She only smiled.

"You've never heard of me, have you?"

"Should I have? Are you some kind of celebrity?"

He gaped at her. "Don't you read the financial pages? See the most eligible bachelor section of any Boston magazine? I'm not a movie star but I'm kind of well known in Boston."

"Never heard of you until we were contacted by Ginny's attorney." She lifted Bella and tickled her belly with her nose. "Look, I get it that you're some big-deal financial guy. And that's cool, but I don't keep up on that stuff."

He said, "Whatever," brushing her off, but his heart beat out a strange tattoo. It was the first time since he'd gotten rich that he met someone who didn't know the details of who he was. He might have thought it would be insulting. Instead, it felt strangely liberating.

"I'm going to take her upstairs while I change." Light and happy, Claire's voice drifted over to him. "Now that her tummy's full, she may go down for a nap, which will give us time to call the nanny service."

His stomach plummeted. The nanny service. That explained the happiness. As soon as he officially hired help, she got to go home.

Annoyance zinged through him, making him snippy. She might be glad to be leaving, but she didn't have to be so obvious about it. "I guess I may be doing some apologizing since you hung up on the service I called last night."

She rose with a laugh. "Or we could just call a different service."

"I thought you said that was the best one?"

"That one's the best, but the other two aren't too far behind. We'll decide which to call when I get downstairs."

She left the kitchen and he found a bowl and a box of cereal. By the time she returned, he'd eaten and read the morning paper.

She set the baby monitor on the table. The small screen above the little speaker showed Bella sound asleep in her crib.

"I thought that needed to stay in her room."

"The camera and microphone are in the room. The screen and speaker go where we go." She sighed. "It took me a little longer to get her to sleep than I'd expected."

He set the paper aside, trying to be nonchalant about the fact that the cute jeans she'd changed into had set his heart to humming again and her desire to go home annoyed him. He shouldn't want her to stay. He should be glad she was going. So that's how he acted. Cool. Casual. Unconcerned that she was leaving.

"Give me a minute to get into some clothes and we'll call the nanny service." He headed for the door, but stopped. Just because he was annoyed that didn't give him license to be a bad host.

"Have you eaten?"

"No, but a cup of coffee will be enough."

He frowned. "Really, Ms. Kincaid. A professional like you should know a good breakfast is necessary."

She laughed. "Yeah. I should know. But I'm not much of a breakfast person."

She turned, opened a cupboard, grabbed a mug and poured herself a cup of coffee.

Matt stood watching her, mesmerized. She was so casual around him, and his home, that the place didn't feel so…sterile. Maybe that's why he didn't want her to leave? Even filled with people, his house never felt like a home.

He shook his head. Now where the hell were his thoughts going? He had to stop this.

He turned away from the sight of her sipping her coffee and left the kitchen.

In his closet, ridiculously, he stared at the clothes. She made simple jeans and a T-shirt look good. It wasn't that he felt he needed to one-up her. He didn't even feel he should be trying to entice her. But he had the strangest urge to look really good.

Irritated with himself for thinking such weird things, he grabbed jeans and a T-shirt and put them on. God only knew why this woman made him think like this. But he wasn't falling victim. He refused.

He found her in the kitchen reading the same paper he had read while she was with Bella. "Ready?"

She snagged the baby monitor as she rose. "As ready as I'll ever be."

Finally. A little sadness in her voice. Not that he wanted her to stay. He was sure he and Bella would be fine once they got a nanny. It was simply insulting that she was so eager to bustle away. He knew her sadness probably stemmed from not wanting to leave Bella. But that pleased him more than thinking she didn't want to leave him. Bella was a baby who needed all the love and affection she could get. He was a grown man who could find himself a new sex partner and be happy—

He frowned. Now, why did that suddenly seem tawdry? Unappealing?

She met him at the door. Holding the baby monitor in one hand as she slid the other into the back pocket of her jeans, she looked up at him. "The business cards are still in the den?"

His mouth went dry. Putting her hand behind her back caused her breasts to punch out, just slightly. But enough to bring his gaze there. He followed the path of a neat little pink T-shirt that hugged her trim waist and fell short of meeting the waistband of her low-rise jeans, exposing an enticing strip of pink skin.

"Well?"

His gaze jumped to hers. "Huh?"

"The business cards? Are they in the den?"

"Um. Yes." Praying to God she hadn't seen the direction of his gaze, but knowing she'd have to be blind to have missed it, he pushed on the swinging door and headed down the hall.

In his office, she set the monitor on the desk between them as he picked up the business cards she'd given him the day before.

If it killed him, he intended to get his cool back. "Okay, agency number one is out for now, since you hung up on them."

She sniffed and looked away.

"So we're on to agency two."

He dialed the first three numbers on the landline on his desk and suddenly a squawk came from the monitor. He glanced at the screen and saw Bella pulling herself into a sitting position as she sobbed.

Claire rose. Motioning with her hand, she said, "You keep going. I'll get her. She probably needs a diaper change."

He winced at the thought of changing a diaper, but replaced the receiver back in its cradle. "No. I'm taking advantage of as much time as I can to learn what I need to learn. I'm not sitting on the sidelines. I haven't changed a diaper yet and while you're here I'd like to do that."

"I think that's a great idea."

In Bella's bedroom, she held back while he approached the crib. Bella sobbed, her little arms raised as if begging for someone to hold her.

"I'm here," he said, feeling the full weight of that. He was here. He would care for her. He would do this.

But when he lifted her into his arms, she didn't settle. She wiped her wet face on the shoulder of his shirt, but still screamed as if the hounds of hell were chasing her.

"Shh. Shh. Bella, it's okay," he crooned, taking a few steps, rocking a bit to comfort her, but she kept crying.

Then she saw Claire. She stretched toward her, wailing like a banshee.

Claire caught his gaze. "May I?"

He levered Bella over to her. "Please."

Bella wrapped her arms around Claire's neck as if she'd found a lifeline.

"I guess she didn't wake up because she needed a diaper."

Claire sniffed a laugh. "No. I think she might have had a bad dream." She rubbed her nose against Bella's face. "Hey, sweetie. It's okay. Don't cry. I have you."

Her crying subsided a bit, but she curled into Claire as if trying to get inside her skin. As if she was afraid of being left.

Matt swallowed. She *was* afraid of being left. She'd lost both of her parents five days ago. Then she'd been put into Claire's custody and Claire had become her anchor.

Bella hadn't slept through the night because she trusted Matt or even because she liked her new crib. She'd slept through the night because she was finally growing accustomed to Claire.

And Claire was leaving.

He scrubbed his hand across his mouth, unsure of what

to do. He hated to see Bella cry but he also hated being dependent upon Claire. She had a life. She was leaving.

He stepped forward, took the baby from Claire's arms. "Hey," he said, then—against every male instinct in his body—he sucked in a breath and did what he had to do. He danced her around in a big sweeping waltz step. "There's no need to cry."

As if by magic, Bella stopped crying, but Claire laughed. "You're dancing."

No kidding. Humiliation and embarrassment buffeted him, but he ignored them. "It's not a big deal," he said, though he knew it was. He probably looked like an idiot. "We've done this before."

"You have?"

"Yes. Yesterday, before you got here, I discovered dancing keeps her quiet."

"I discovered it the first night I had her."

A little more comfortable, Matt waltzed her around the room again. "She likes it."

"Maybe her mom danced with her?"

He stopped. Sadness made his stomach plummet. "Maybe she did."

She caught his gaze. "Don't take that the wrong way. It's nice for Bella to have that connection."

"It's good to remind her of her mom?"

"I don't think she thinks of her mom. I think she associates the dancing with love."

His heart froze in his chest. He looked from Claire to Bella and back to Claire again. "Dancing makes her feel loved."

"That's what I'm guessing."

"Then we'll dance."

CHAPTER SEVEN

TEN minutes later, Claire carried Bella to Matt's office, an odd feeling in her stomach. For as much of a big, strong, stubborn guy as Matt Patterson was, he really wanted to do what was right for this baby. He genuinely wanted to be a good daddy. He didn't mind looking a bit silly. And he wanted to learn.

She sat on the chair in front of the desk as Matt dialed the number for the nanny service.

"Hello, this is Matt Patterson. May I speak with Mary Mahoney?"

He sat in silence, waiting to be transferred, while Claire straightened the collar on Bella's pale green one-piece pajama. "You look especially pretty in green."

As if she understood the compliment, Bella grinned at her, but her little blue eyes were red from crying and still watery. Claire's heart twisted. In an hour or so they'd put her down for a nap again, then the temporary nanny would arrive, Claire would leave and Bella would wake up to two people she considered strangers. Plus, there was no guarantee that the nanny would teach Matt. Or even let him spend any quality time with Bella. Or let him dance.

If Matt knew more about babies, he could stand his ground with a stern nanny. But as unconfident as he was now, he'd let a nanny take over. And Bella would lose her daddy.

Suddenly Matt straightened in his chair. "Hello. Yes. Ms. Mahoney. I'm Matt Patterson. I recently got custody—"

She pressed her fingers on the button in the cradle for the phone receiver and disconnected the call.

He gaped at her. "Are you trying to make me look like an idiot?"

"No." She hugged cuddly Bella to her, swept her lips across her downy hair. "But I think it might be premature to leave Bella with a nanny. I think what we need to do is have me stay another day so she can get more adjusted to you."

He slowly replaced the phone receiver in its cradle. "You want to stay?"

Refusing to meet his gaze, she fussed with Bella's pajamas again. "I wouldn't say I *want* to stay, but I think I *need* to stay for Bella's sake."

"I can't say it's a bad idea, but you might want to mention these things to me before I call someone, instead of just hanging up the phone when I'm talking."

She winced. "Sorry." She said it casually, but the full ramifications of what she'd done by hanging up the phone began to sink in. She'd slept in a bedroom next to his the night before. True, she'd closed the door, but she was still in his house. And they'd kissed—because they were attracted. True, they'd talked that out. They weren't suited. So they were avoiding or ignoring that attraction.

But what if something happened that they couldn't? What if they kissed again? What if he wanted to do more than kiss? Could she resist him?

She mentally shook herself. Of course she could resist

him. She'd been resisting men for five years—*men she hadn't been attracted to.*

She peeked up at Matt. Strong shoulders. Handsome face. Sexy eyes.

She'd be spending another whole day with him…sleeping next to his bedroom again—

Oh, boy.

Studying her across the desk, he leaned back in his chair. "So what do we do now?"

The smart thing to do would be to keep them so focused on Bella and so busy she could forget this ridiculous attraction. Especially since he didn't seem to be having the same trepidation about it that she was. "You said you wanted to learn a few more things before a nanny completely takes over. Why don't we spend today doing some of that?"

He sat up. "Okay."

Trying to be nonchalant, she said, "Too bad she doesn't need a diaper change, since you danced instead of changed her diaper the last time she cried."

He sniffed a laugh.

The room got quiet.

The urge to run bubbled up in her, but she gathered her courage. After all, she was doing this for Bella.

"So since she doesn't need a diaper, has already been fed and doesn't want to sleep…maybe we should play."

He glanced over. "Play?"

"Sure." She rose, walked the baby to the thick Oriental rug in front of the sofa and lowered herself and Bella to the floor. "Babies are naturally curious. So sometimes playing can be as simple as setting her on the floor and letting her explore."

He ambled over. "And how do I fit into this equation?"

"You keep her from getting hurt, as you point out things that might be fun for her."

He sat on the floor beside her. "Like what?"

She peered around. There wasn't a damned thing in his house that might interest a baby. Worse, sitting on the floor with him only inches away, sprawled out comfortably, caused weird feelings to ripple through her. This was how he'd be with Bella. A sort of clueless but affable dad. He'd be sweet. Loving.

Great. Adding emotion to her attraction had been real smart.

She popped up off the floor. Seeing him as a good dad upped his likability by about a thousand percent. If she wasn't careful, she wouldn't just be fighting a sexual attraction; she'd be falling for another guy who was all wrong for her.

"Maybe I should go upstairs and get her one of the rattles and her bear."

She walked up the spiral staircase and back the hall to his bedroom, then took a deep breath as she leaned against the closed door.

She was fine. There was nothing to worry about. She'd learned her lesson about falling for self-absorbed men. She wasn't in any danger of losing her heart. Even thinking that was stupid. She'd agreed to stay for Bella. Bella needed a real daddy, not just a guy who paid for a nanny. She needed a daddy who would play with her when he came home from work, tuck her in at night, kiss her forehead. And she could teach him to do all that, if she kept her wits about her. It might be a little uncomfortable for her and she might have to miss work—

Miss work! She hadn't told her boss she would be taking time off!

She raced to her purse and retrieved her cell phone. With one click she speed dialed Joni's number.

"Dysart Adoptions."

"Oh, my gosh! Joni! I'm so sorry! I forgot all about you."

Joni, the owner of the adoption agency, chuckled. "That's okay. I figured you were busy with Bella."

"I was." She winced. "I *am*. Matt Patterson's staff are all on vacation so I volunteered to help him."

"Oh?"

"We were just walking back to the den to contact a nanny service when Bella woke up from her morning nap and she was inconsolable."

"Poor thing!"

"I know. The sweet baby is having so much trouble adjusting. Matt grabbed her out of the crib and it didn't even slow her down. But when she saw me, she reached for me and cuddled in and pretty soon she was calm."

"She's gotten accustomed to you."

"Yes."

"And you're not ready to leave her."

"I can't leave her like this. Plus, once she was calm, Matt took her and danced with her."

"Danced with her?"

"It calms her. I didn't tell him. He figured it out for himself. I can see he has the potential to be a really great dad. In a few days, I could teach him so much and then he would be comfortable around the baby and wouldn't desert her to a nanny when he gets one."

"You think he has the potential to get so accustomed to Bella that he'd spend time with her?"

"Yes. There's just something about the way he deals with her that makes me see he wants this. He *wants* to be a good dad. And if I can help him, I think I should." She paused, bit her bottom lip. "You're okay with me staying the rest of the week? I'll take it as vacation time."

"It's Tuesday. That's four whole days."

"I know…but Bella needs me."

"I think it's kind of cute."

Her breath stuttered out on a long sigh. "I don't know about cute. I just feel awful for her. She's so small and she can't even talk to tell us how she feels. And Matt genuinely wants to be a good dad. Right now, he's waiting for the right moment to learn how to change a diaper."

Joni laughed.

"Okay. I've got to run. I left her on the floor of a den that looks like it could be part of a museum."

Joni's voice perked up. "Oh, interesting. You're getting a sneak peek at his house!"

"Yes. I am. But I wouldn't want to live here. Everything's perfect. And I think that's going to be hard on Bella, too. While I'm here I might just suggest he create a few baby-friendly rooms."

"Well, have fun. And good luck with Bella."

"Thanks."

After disconnecting the call, she removed Bella's bear from the crib and dug through the diaper bag for one of the two rattles. She returned to the den feeling a lot better about her decision to help Matt. Joni didn't see anything wrong with her staying. In fact, she thought it was cute. Because that's the kind of people she and Joni were. They loved kids. Babies especially. They'd dedicated their lives to caring for them. Staying at this house for Bella and teaching Matt to be a good dad wasn't out of line. It was what she did.

As she entered the den, Matt said, "What took you so long?"

"I had to call my boss and arrange for some time off."

He groaned. "Sorry. I forgot about that."

"That's okay. She's fine with me staying a couple more days. In fact, I took the rest of the week off so I can help. We all have Bella's best interests at heart." She glanced around. "By the way…where is she?"

"Under the desk."

"Under the desk!"

"Don't worry. There's nothing under there. And she seems to like it." He smiled briefly. "It reminds me of when my sister Charlotte and I used to sit under my dad's desk and call it a fort."

"A fort?"

"We were always at war with our other sisters." He paused.

Knowing family was a sensitive subject for him and not wanting to get him in another bad mood, she ignored that last comment and went in search of Bella.

After moving the office chair out of the way, she stooped in front of the entry to the desk. "What are you doing?"

Bella screeched happily and patted her chubby thighs.

"Oh, so you do like it under there?"

She squealed with delight.

Claire raised her head until she could see above the desk. Catching Matt's gaze, she said, "Come over. Play with her." She waved the bear. "I have props."

He hoisted himself off the floor and strolled over. "Props?"

"The bear and the rattle. Things that will make playing easier."

He snorted a laugh, but slid the tall-backed chair far enough away from the desk that he could crouch beside Claire. "Hey, Bella."

She gurgled what Claire surmised equaled hello in baby talk.

"So, this is how the tiny half lives."

Bella laughed.

Claire turned a bit to face him. "She likes you. She really does. She just needs to get accustomed to you."

"And that will require me sitting on the floor a lot?"

"Among other things."

He shook his head, once again getting comfortable on the floor, laying out as he had on the Oriental rug in front of the sofa. "You know, I'm glad you don't know me. Because I have no reputation with you, I don't have to worry about ruining it by doing foolish things like sitting on the floor."

She looked away. How would he feel if he knew that the things he considered foolish like laying out on the floor actually made him more attractive to her?

She shifted the conversation back to Bella, the reason she'd stayed. "You also don't have a reputation to ruin with Bella. No matter what you do, this baby will love you." She reached in and tickled Bella's tummy. "Just as you are."

The idea that someone could love him just as he was stopped Matt cold. He peeked under the desk, at the little girl happily gurgling as if she'd found heaven. He scooted a little closer, looked at Bella with new eyes. Not as a baby who needed *his* protection, but as someone who would love *him*.

Just as he was.

Nobody had ever loved him just as he was. Even Ginny wanted him to change. That was why they'd divorced. She'd wanted a more attentive, loving husband. He'd been as closed off as a man could get. And even when he tried to be more honest, more receptive, he couldn't take those final steps.

He peeked at Claire. "No matter what I do…she'll love me?"

Claire smiled. "Yes. As long as you love her."

"I've never really been good at love."

She shrugged. "There is no such thing as good or bad in love. There's just love. If you love this little girl, she will know it and she will respond."

Bella cooed with happiness. He imagined her first birthday, imagined her learning to walk, learning to talk, turning to him for help and guidance and affection. And hugging him. Returning the love and affection he gave her.

Unimaginable warmth filled him. Along with a mountain of regret.

He swallowed hard. "I didn't really love her mom the way she needed to be loved."

"Obviously, you did something right. She left her child in your care."

"What I did right was stay friends with her." He peeked over at Claire. "And her new husband. Oswald was a great guy. A smart guy. But he always just missed the boat when it came to the big deals. So I let him sell me this house." He glanced around at it. "And having both the sale of this house and a sale to me to put on his résumé gave him the leg up he needed. When he…" He swallowed, unable to say *died*. Instead, he said, "This time last week he was one of the biggest real-estate brokers in Boston."

She put a comforting hand on his arm. "That's a great story."

"That's the only reason my ex-wife stayed friends with me. I felt I owed her so I helped her new husband. I considered the score settled. They felt I'd gone above and beyond the call of duty and made me their new best friend."

Claire shook her head. "You're so down on yourself. Did you ever stop to think that maybe they liked you?"

"Wall Street's Iceman? The guy who broke Ginny's heart?" He snorted a laugh. "I doubt it."

"I think you're selling yourself short."

There she was again, seeing the good in him. She didn't understand how cool and distant he was, even though she'd said she did after their kiss at her apartment. He had to remind her she wasn't magically going to find his nice side, or she would get hurt.

He caught Claire's gaze. "I loved my ex-wife. I truly did. But being dedicated to work, I ignored her. She had seen I wasn't capable of real love and she moved on. I didn't fault her for that. I didn't blame her. But she knew me. The real me. The me who doesn't love."

Claire ran a finger down Bella's chubby arm, making the baby giggle. "Look at this sweet child. Do you really believe your ex-wife would have left her in your care if she genuinely believed you were incapable of loving her?"

"Maybe she left Bella with me because I have money enough to get her a good nanny, buy her everything she needs, see that she gets into a good university."

Claire gasped, clearly offended by his interpretation of Ginny's motives. "That's not how moms think! More than money, more than nannies, more than grand houses and fancy educations, babies need love. Mommies know that. Ginny wouldn't have left Bella in your care if she believed you couldn't love her."

Real fear tightened Matt's chest. He could care for this baby. He could give her affection. Giving her affection seemed to come naturally. But real love? That wasn't in the cards. Ginny would have known that.

"Ginny didn't believe I could love. She made me guardian only because she needed a name to put in her will. She never suspected she was going to die. Otherwise, she would have thought this through—found someone better to raise her daughter."

His solid, certain voice could have convinced Claire he was right...except she knew moms. They did not leave their babies with just anyone. They didn't make guardianship decisions lightly. Unfortunately, he wasn't in the mood to hear that, so she didn't reply.

Still, looking at him, reclining on the floor, watching the baby under his desk, waiting for his chance to learn how to change a diaper, she frowned. Very few people probably saw him this relaxed, but his ex-wife would have. She would have been with him in all kinds of situations and would have known him better than anybody ever had.

Ginny had to have seen something in him that nobody else saw.

And if she did see Matt as a man capable of loving a little girl enough to raise her, what would it take to bring out whatever Ginny had seen in him?

She didn't know. But the part of her that loved Bella knew she had to figure that out. She had the rest of the week. Plenty of time to push him a bit. But later. When he'd be a bit more receptive. There were lots of other, less threatening, less personal things they could discuss now to relax him. Get him to trust her. Before she began probing for whatever it was Ginny had seen in him.

"Speaking of big fancy houses not being what babies need, you might want to make a few kid-friendly places for Bella."

He glanced over. "Kid-friendly?"

"I think you'll need a playroom for her. You'll probably want a big family room…somewhere the two of you can play board games or video games and watch TV."

"Maybe foosball? Or ping pong."

"Sure. Whatever you want. Your best conversations with her will happen while you're doing something else."

"Makes sense."

The room got quiet. Bella happily sucked on her rattle. Claire once again searched her brain for something Bella-related to discuss, and realized he'd never made firm plans about his trip the following week. If he would be taking Bella to Texas, then teaching him how to travel with a baby ranked almost as high as demonstrating how to change a diaper.

"So what about the reunion in Texas? You said you might not go."

He sighed. "I have to go. I promised my sisters, Ellie, Charlotte and Alex."

"Ah." So he would need help.

"Don't make too much of that."

"That's okay. I'm not interested in your family as much as I am in helping you plan for the trip. You're probably going to need a baby carrier and lots more clothes."

He shrugged. "The temporary nanny should be able to help me with that, though, right?"

Her cheeks heated. Why did she keep forgetting he'd be replacing her? Was it because she wanted to see him raise Bella on his own—or because she couldn't stand the thought of being replaced?

She glanced at sweet Bella and her heart melted. But when she moved her gaze to Matt, her stomach tumbled. He saw himself as such a terrible person, yet here he lay, on the floor, just to be with Bella. To give her time to get accustomed to him.

How was a woman supposed to resist a guy like that?

"Yes. The nanny will take care of most of that." Fumbling for something to say to get her mind off how irresistible he became every time he was good to Bella, she inadvertently took them back to family again. "I think it will be good for Bella to get out among your family."

"Family is the group who taught me that it's best to never show your soft side."

"Really? I'd love to have a sister or brother." She smiled wistfully. "A sister to confide in. A brother to defend me… or for me to look up to."

"You can have my sister Alex. She's a chatterbox. And I hear I have a half brother Holt. You can have him, too. He's supposedly somebody everybody looks up to."

Her eyes widened. "You don't know if your own brother is somebody everybody looks up to?"

"I don't want to know!"

His shouted words echoed around the room. Embarrassment flooded Claire's entire body. He might be sweet and sexy when he was caring for Bella, but *this* was the real Matt Patterson.

What had he called himself? Iceman?

No matter what Ginny had seen in him, he was an iceman.

She rose. "You know, suddenly I am hungry. I think I'll just go to the kitchen and see if I can scout out something for breakfast."

He blew his breath out on a sigh. "Can you take the baby with you? I have some overseas calls to make."

She smiled politely and said, "Sure," but his request that she take the baby with her was another reminder that he wasn't a sweet guy, grappling with caring for a baby. He was a rich man, accustomed to people doing his bidding. He didn't *like* her. He might be attracted to her, but he saw her as an employee, a servant. He might also want to be a good dad for Bella, but he had a business to run and that was his priority.

She left the room, Bella on her arm. Matt hoisted himself from the floor and plopped down into the tall-backed chair. When Ellie had first told him about this family reunion, he wasn't interested, but when Alex and then Charlotte also started to pester him about it, he agreed to go. Especially for Charlotte. Because he liked her. Because she could persuade him to do things he didn't really want to do. Even when the ramifications of what he'd agreed to do had settled in, he'd decided he could go, be his cool, aloof self and then just come home and forget all about Texas and his real dad and the four half siblings he didn't need.

But now he had Bella. A baby. Because Ginny, the ex-wife who'd become a real friend to him after their divorce, had died. Grief rumbled in his chest, squeezing his heart. It came with a heaviness he couldn't even define or describe. He felt more for the wife who had dumped him than the pack of family he had but really didn't know. It didn't seem right to be off meeting them, as if nothing had happened, when Ginny was dead.

He was sorry he'd yelled at Claire. But she didn't get it. Not having a family, she didn't realize that real families weren't warm and fuzzy. Siblings were competitive. Parents could hold grudges. Hurts could run deep. And getting a baby to raise wasn't a gift from the heavens. It was a responsibility.

He leaned back in his chair, but bounced forward again. The best way to forget about his personal life was to work. He picked up the phone receiver, dialed a number and got his mind where it needed to be. On business.

He talked with two banks and four prospective investors for his latest venture. Twenty minutes later, the office door opened and Claire haltingly stepped inside. "My boss called. I have to go to work. Just for an hour or so to debrief her on some cases she'll need to handle for me tomorrow. But I'll be back."

The fact that she would still stay after he'd yelled at her humbled him. It was no wonder she thought there were good people in the world. She was one of them.

"Okay. Thanks."

She motioned toward the ceiling. "Bella's upstairs in her crib...asleep."

He nodded, wishing she'd just leave because he was feeling weird things about her, too. Wondering why she was so nice to a guy who was nothing but snippy with her. Wondering why she was alone, not married, and remembering the bad relationship in her past that she'd mentioned but not really explained. Wondering why he kept thinking about her, when he shouldn't care. When he should have let her leave that morning.

He said, "Thanks." But a vision of Bella waking, screaming for Claire, filled him, and he remembered why he hadn't let her leave. He couldn't care for Bella. Oh, he knew the basics, he could even dance with her to quiet her, but so far Claire was the one Bella really wanted. And he hadn't yet changed a diaper or fed her. Dancing wouldn't help if her pants were wet and her tummy empty.

He swallowed a lump in his throat that felt very much like his pride. "What do I do if she wakes up?"

She took a few more careful steps into the room. "She should sleep the entire time I'm gone. But if she doesn't, change her diaper, give her a bottle and play with her like we did this morning."

He nodded, but she wouldn't look at him. She kept her gaze focused on the floor.

Heat swamped him. He hadn't meant to be so angry with her. After all, his family wasn't her fault.

"You might want to get Jimmy to help you set up the play yard and swing we bought yesterday afternoon with the crib. She'll love the swing. It will definitely settle her if you can't get her to stop crying."

He said, "Thanks," wishing she'd just meet his gaze, knowing he didn't deserve a smile. But she turned and left the room.

He tossed his pencil to his desk. *This* was why he hated dealing with people, and the truth of why he didn't want to go to Texas. Alone in London, with too much time to think about things, he'd begun to wonder if maybe his problem with his extended family wasn't the fault of his seven siblings but his.

Maybe *he* was the reason the whole damned family couldn't get along. After all, *he* and his twin, Ellie, contributed to the reason his mother had left Texas. At least, that was what Cedric had told him the night of their big fight. Had his mother not gotten pregnant, she might have been able to handle living in Texas. But having twins in a rural county, so far away from her family, had made her run.

Claire left Matt's house, grateful for an hour alone in her car, even if she was fighting traffic.

When she arrived at Dysart Adoptions, she immediately walked back to Joni's office.

"Hey."

Blond-haired, blue-eyed Joni looked up. "Hey! I'm glad you could come in."

She winced. "I'm sorry I dumped everything on you without any notice."

Joni motioned for her to sit. "It's not like we're really

busy. I just hate to see you wasting your vacation on something that's essentially work."

"I know. But Bella's special and in a way so is Matt. He wants to be a good dad so much that he can't hide it. But he's more than a bit rough around the edges." She slid to the seat in front of Joni's desk. "Did you know his nickname on Wall Street is Iceman?"

Joni's face fell. "How awful for Bella."

"Well, that's just it. I'd think how awful for Bella, if I didn't keep getting glimpses of a nice guy underneath his Iceman exterior."

Joni laughed, but her laughter quickly died. "Oh. Wait." She studied Claire for a second, then said, "You're not falling for him, are you?"

Claire sat up in her chair. "Absolutely not." She'd had this conversation with herself in the car driving to the adoption agency. And convinced herself she hadn't gotten angry that he'd yelled at her; she'd gotten angry that he hadn't learned to control his temper around the baby. "Number one, he's so far out of my league I'd be crazy to even consider it. Number two, I'm literally teaching this guy how to love. He says he hurt his ex-wife so badly he had to make it up to her by helping her new husband with a business deal. And he can't understand why Ginny would leave her daughter in his care when she above everybody else knows he can't love. I'd be *crazy* to get involved with him."

Joni said, "Okay. Good."

"I mean, it's not like the guy doesn't have potential. If I'm reading the situation right, I think he had a very soft heart at one time and something happened in his family that broke it. I'm guessing his Iceman image is a defensive wall to keep him from getting hurt again. Which is why I think there's lots of hope for him with Bella."

Joni inclined her head. "That makes sense." She caught Claire's gaze. "As long as you're only working to repair his heart enough to raise a baby, not because you want something to happen between you two."

"I already said I don't want anything to happen between us."

"Because bringing him far enough along that he'd be able to love you—as well as a baby—would be a big job."

"I know."

"And it would probably end up with you getting hurt."

"I know that, too."

"Just checking."

Joni dropped the subject after that and they went to work on quickly reviewing the few cases Claire had on her desk. But when she left Dysart Adoptions, Joni's words rolled around in her head.

She could probably teach Matt enough to care for Bella in a day or two. She hadn't needed to take the whole week off.

Was she subconsciously trying to heal him for herself?

Did she think she could be the woman of his dreams?

CHAPTER EIGHT

When Claire returned, she found Matt in the kitchen, making lunch. Bella sat in the high chair, banging a rattle on the tray. Matt stood at the grill beside the stainless-steel stove.

"Are those grilled cheese sandwiches I smell?"

"Yes."

She shrugged out of her coat. "Really?"

He glanced over, then turned his attention back to his sandwiches. His voice was chilly as the ocean in January when he said, "I can cook. I wasn't always rich."

"Ah."

"My stepfather was rich. And yes, I grew up in the lap of luxury, but I had to put myself through school. I got a job, lived in a rat hole of an apartment and paid enough tuition to put a new wing on the library just to get a basic bachelor's degree."

Unable to stop herself, she laughed. "Why would you want to live in a rat hole of an apartment if your family was rich?"

"I had a falling-out with my stepfather." His voice wavered a bit, as if he didn't want to answer, but he had.

She hung her coat across the back of a chair. Combining the conversation she'd had with Joni to this revelation, she knew it was time to tread lightly. She'd been pushing him to be sweet, to be nice, to be *honest,* for Bella's sake, and it finally dawned on her how hard that might be for him. He was a guy so accustomed to getting his own way that he'd rather pay his tuition himself and live in a rat hole than make up with his stepfather. And here she was forcing him to buckle under for everything she wanted.

Of course, she was doing it for Bella.

She ambled toward the grill. She continually pushed him because Bella needed good care, but she didn't have to be a shrew. She pointed at the sandwiches. "You wouldn't want to share those, would you?"

"If my mother taught me anything, it was to share. I'm a great host."

"I'd set the table as repayment."

"I suppose that could be a deal."

"Great."

She rummaged until she found plates and cups, set the table and made a pot of coffee. He heated soup to go with the sandwiches and they sat at the table to eat, with Bella happily chattering in the high chair beside them.

"So how does a preppy boy survive living in a rat hole?"

He stopped his spoon halfway to his mouth. His lips quirked a bit. "Not easily."

"I can imagine."

"I don't think you can. I'd never actually seen a bug indoors before, so cockroaches scared the hell out of me."

She burst out laughing. "Good grief!"

"The walls of my apartment were paper thin. I froze in the winter and sweltered in the summer." He smiled, almost wistfully. "It certainly taught me a lot about life." He caught her gaze. "Real life. Not the sheltered existence I had as Cedric Patterson's son."

"I'll bet." She cocked her head. If he'd survived that,

learning to care for Bella should be a piece of cake. But now wasn't the time to remind him of that. They were making up after their argument and she would do her part. She would share a little about herself, too, so he wouldn't feel he was always the one giving. "I actually did about the same thing."

He frowned. "Really? You left the lap of luxury for a rat hole?"

"Maybe not the lap of luxury, but a very comfortable home. I was angry with my dad because he just never seemed to want me around, so I refused to take his money for tuition." She shook her head. "Actually, that's not totally true. I never asked him for money for tuition to see if he'd remember that I needed it. He didn't. All the deadlines passed and suddenly I had a twenty-thousand-dollar tuition bill that needed to be paid immediately and no money. And I was too angry to ask my dad to please remember he had a daughter."

Matt's face softened as he said, "What did you do?"

"I went to the bank and withdrew my savings and paid it."

"Ouch."

"At least I had savings. I had the first semester's tuition and enough for a good bit of the second semester, but I was furious. He never even considered that I'd need money. I was getting an allowance, but it wasn't enough for tuition and books and the dorm. Just basics like one meal a day and shampoo. And I realized he didn't even care about me to ask." She swallowed back the wave of emotion that clogged her throat. "So I decided the hell with him and I went job hunting."

"That's when you became a nanny."

"Yep. Changed my classes to night classes and lived in

with the families I worked for so I didn't have to worry about the dorm. And became my own woman."

His brow furrowed. "So, we're sort of alike."

"A little, but my story doesn't end as happily as yours."

He sent her a look, encouraging her to explain. Unsure if she should, she sucked in a breath. But in the end, she decided that if she intended to push him past his boundaries, the least she could do was be honest with him.

"My dad died my third year at university. All the money he made, all the money that kept him from me, meant nothing. He had a heart attack when he was alone and, with no one to help him or even call an ambulance, he died."

Matt reached across the table and covered her hand with his. "I'm so sorry."

"If he'd paid one whit of attention to me, I would have been there. He wouldn't have died. But he'd treated me like an afterthought and I genuinely believed he didn't want me around." Bottled up feelings began to pop free, making her voice shaky and her eyes water. "But do you want to know the real punch line of this story? All his money came to me. All that money that kept him from me." She paused to take a cleansing breath. "I didn't want it. But I wasn't so foolish as to flush it down a toilet."

He barked a short laugh, one of acknowledgment, but with very little humor.

"I bought a new car and my condo and gave the rest to charity."

He studied her from across the table. "You gave your inheritance to charity?"

"I didn't want it. I took enough for a decent start on life, then let it go. I didn't want the money that had stolen my dad from me."

"And that's why you're not impressed with money."

She inclined her head, not able to speak. Now she wasn't just remembering her time at university. Memories of her lonely years as a little girl had also floated to the surface. Memories of how much she'd wanted her father's love, and how stubborn she'd gotten as a teenager, staying out of the house on weekends that she'd known he'd be home because she feared he'd only spend his time working and ignore her. And she couldn't handle the pain of his silent rejection anymore.

Tears filled her eyes and the lump of emotion came back to her throat. She missed her dad. But, then again, it seemed she'd spent her whole life missing her dad.

"That's why you want me to be a good dad for Bella."

She nodded.

He pulled his hand away and scrubbed it down his face. "I'm sorry."

"I'm sorry, too." Her voice broke. They were finally genuinely getting to know each other. He wasn't apologizing for bringing up a sensitive subject any more than she was apologizing for getting hurt over his sniping at her. Their apologies were for their misconceptions about each other up to this point. All the same, it was the first time she'd spoken about her dad with anyone and emotions she hadn't expected overwhelmed her.

"Sometimes I look back on the years I was in school being stubborn and headstrong over my dad's 'slights' and I realize that if I'd pushed for his attention things might have been very different."

To her embarrassment, her tears spilled over. She'd cried about her dad before, but never so honestly and certainly never with another person. But she could talk about this with Matt because she knew he understood. He hadn't gotten along with his stepfather any better than she'd gotten along with her father. But that didn't make it hurt any less. It also didn't take away the guilt. She'd been twenty-one when her dad died. Surely, she could have been mature enough to go to his house and say, "Let's have dinner?"

Fresh tears erupted at that and she rose from the table to get something to wipe her eyes. After a few seconds of searching for tissues, her frustration with looking collided with her frustration with her life and her tears became full-scale sobbing. "Is there a box of tissues in this room that seems to have everything but tissues?"

Panicked by her tears, he bounced off his seat. "That's a good question." He roamed around the room, fruitlessly seeking tissues, and in the end ripped a paper towel off the roll by the sink.

But when he reached her, she wouldn't look at him again, reminding him of how she wouldn't look at him after he'd yelled about not wanting to know his family. Regret filled him, along with intense longing to be kind to this woman who'd had a childhood far more difficult than his.

Rather than hand the paper towel to her, he rolled it in a ball and lightly dabbed it along the tracks of her tears.

That brought her gaze to his and he swallowed. She was so beautiful, but right in that moment it wasn't her beauty that called to him. It was something more, something deeper, something so important he didn't dare let himself examine it.

But he also couldn't ignore it. With their gazes locked and tears welling in her eyes again, that "something deeper" inside him wouldn't let this moment slide away. He lowered his head, watching her eyes darken. With fear? With curiosity? He couldn't tell. He only knew that if he didn't kiss her right this second, he would be sorry.

Softly, slowly, he let his lips graze hers, telling her with his actions that he understood and wanted to comfort her.

And every bit as slowly her lips rose to meet his, answering him, accepting his comfort.

The kiss grew as they experimented with the feel and taste of each other's lips. Arousal surged through him, along with the knowledge that she wasn't like any other woman he'd ever known. Not even Ginny, a pampered princess who might have had to fight alongside her second husband for success, but who didn't understand suffering. Sadness. The feeling of not quite living up to the expectations of the person who meant the most to you.

Claire understood. She was a real person. A real woman. Someone with problems and goals, who knew life didn't always turn out the way you hoped.

She suddenly pulled away from him. "What are you doing?"

She stepped back, gaping at him as if he were crazy. "You told me you're a mean, coldhearted playboy. Somebody I should stay away from. Why the hell would you kiss me like that?"

Like that. She hadn't spelled it out, but he knew what she meant. Why had he kissed her like he meant it? Like he had feelings for her. Like they had connected.

His breath caught in his chest and seemed to knot there. What the hell was he doing?

"I need to wash my face." She took another step back, then turned and raced out of the kitchen.

He rubbed his hand across the back of his neck as he sat at the table again. Vibrating with confusion, he stared at his soup. He couldn't argue her logic. Didn't want to apologize. How could he? What would he say? *Hey, we connected. Why not kiss?* He wasn't like that. He didn't want to be like that! He wanted to be left alone.

Yet she needed him. He more than sensed it. And something inside of him surged with longing to be the one to fix whatever was wrong.

It was absurd. Not just because he'd never wanted to be a great "fixer" of people. He was an iceman. But also because he didn't know how to fix anybody. Hell, he couldn't even fix himself.

Racing up the stairs to the makeshift nursery, Claire just wanted to roll up in a ball and die. She didn't know what was worse, exposing her secrets to a virtual stranger, or accepting his comfort when she knew deep down inside he didn't mean it.

Oh, for a few seconds she thought he had. The sweet, sensitive way he'd kissed her made her believe her story had touched him. And maybe it had, but it didn't mean anything. He was who he was. And by God, she'd promised herself and Joni she wasn't going to try to change him.

Yet, the second his lips touched hers, her common sense fled out the window!

What the hell was she thinking? They might have a lot of things from their pasts in common, but how long had she known this guy? Twenty-four hours? Only an idiot didn't learn from her mistakes. And she'd made a huge mistake at university with Ben, a professor she barely knew. She would not make that mistake again. Especially not with a guy nicknamed Iceman.

She stepped into his bedroom and closed the door with a sigh. They had a huge house at their disposal yet they were virtually sleeping in the same room. Sharing a bathroom. Spending twenty-four hours a day together. Telling secrets they hadn't told another soul. Was it any wonder they were acting out of character?

She splashed water on her face and looked at her reflection in the mirror around the waterfall. This was the danger Joni had warned her about and she'd fluffed off thinking she was strong enough to resist him.

Well, maybe she wasn't.

Loneliness made her vulnerable; longing for a family had made her take a foolish risk with Ben. Being with Matt seemed to bring out her loneliness and her longing and wish for things in him that absolutely weren't there.

Unless she wanted to make another mistake, they had to stop having personal conversations. She had to take this time together and make it all about baby lessons again. No more watching his feelings. No more friendly overtures. Nothing but baby lessons.

When she returned downstairs, he was happily playing with Bella, who still sat in the high chair. As she entered the kitchen, his eyes clouded with regret, which only made her feel worse. If she hadn't blubbered on about her dad, he probably wouldn't have kissed her.

"You're back."

"I told you I just needed to wash my face."

"Look, I'm sorry—"

She stopped him with a wave of her hand. "We're fine. Talking about my dad upset me and I took it out on you."

His eyebrows rose. "Took it out on me?"

"I normally don't freak out when someone kisses me." She drew a breath. "But…" She waited until he met her gaze before she said, "Our circumstances are unusual. We're virtually sleeping in the same room. We're playing house with a baby. I think we need to use a little common sense and not do things like talk about our lives and kiss."

Looking incredibly relieved, he nodded.

They fed Bella as if nothing had happened and carried her back to the nursery. Focusing on the baby, Claire's calm, confident demeanor returned. As Matt went to the dresser for clean pj's, Claire opened Bella's little jeans and stifled a laugh over the sight he'd made of her diaper.

"I should have given you a diaper lesson before I left."

He sniffed. "Maybe."

The tightness in her chest loosened a bit. This was what they needed to do. Focus on Bella. Forget about kissing. Forget about talking. Stop trying to be friends.

She considered offering to give him diaper lessons now, but didn't feel comfortable with them standing so close when they were only a few minutes off a kiss and an argument. Instead, she let him go downstairs for a fresh bottle.

A few minutes later, with Bella asleep in the crib, Matt led her into the office/den. Walking to his desk, he peered back at her. "While you were at your office, I took the liberty of calling a nanny service."

She could have been insulted, thinking he was trying to get rid of her. But after that kiss she wanted to leave.

"Not giving me a chance to hang up on them this time?"

He smiled. "Exactly."

As he sat in the chair behind the desk, she sat on the one in front of it. "So?"

"So...since you're here, I thought I might skip the temporary nanny and I talked with them about hiring someone permanently. They emailed a bunch of résumés and I printed them out."

He reached behind to the printer on the credenza, pulled out a stack of papers and handed them to her. "I'm giving you first right of refusal. Knowing me the way you do, and also knowing Bella, you probably understand better than anyone who won't fit with us."

She took the résumés. "I can weed out the prospective

nannies I think won't work." She glanced up at him. "But you can't choose a nanny from a résumé."

"I'd intended to interview them."

She nodded. "Good."

He pointed across the desk at the papers she held. "You pick the ones I should interview."

She looked down at the résumés. Now that their relationship had returned to something more businesslike, her goal for being here—making sure Bella got the best care—guided her again. "If you want, I can help you with the interviews."

"That would be great."

She began reading the résumés, looking specifically for nannies with experience with babies. They called the agency and set up interviews with six of the candidates for Friday.

"So if all goes well," Claire said, rising from her seat. "You should have somebody on Saturday."

Matt tossed his pen to his desk. "Yeah." And then she would go. And then he could stop feeling these odd things he always felt around her.

That was good.

Very good.

Very good for *both* of them.

She made a few marks on the résumés, and he remained in his seat, not really sure if he should stay or go. Luckily, Bella's little voice tumbled from the baby monitor.

He bounced off his seat. "I'll get her."

Claire rose, too. "I'll help. I think it's time for the diaper lesson."

A laugh bubbled up, but he stopped it before it could escape. Even when she was mad at him, she could be funny. And he liked that—a lot more than he cared to admit. But she'd had a rough childhood, and she deserved a good life with a nice guy. He didn't fit that bill. So he had to stop responding to her. Stop laughing. Stop telling her things. In fact, maybe it was time to let her go. He knew a lot about caring for Bella and he wasn't an idiot. Now that he was comfortable with the baby, he could figure out a lot of the rest of it himself. And she'd chosen the best candidates for his nanny. He'd interviewed people before. Surely, he could hire his own nanny.

They walked up the stairs and entered the nursery to find Bella sitting up, her face tearstained, her lips turned down in an angry pout.

"Oh, sweetie," Claire said, lifting Bella from the crib. "You're all right."

Bella nuzzled into Claire's neck, and clung to her, causing Matt's heart to somersault. For as much as he wished he could let Claire leave so he could stop having these "feelings" about her, Bella needed her.

Still, he had to get Bella beyond this. She was his child to raise and he would step up.

He walked over, took Bella from Claire. "Hey—" He almost said *kid,* but wondered if the reason Bella was so slow to bond with him was his direct manner with her. So he said, "Sweetie," as Claire did. "How about if Daddy changes your pants this time?"

She sniffed and turned to Claire, reaching for her, but Claire stepped back as if she understood Matt's intention to spend more time with Bella and speed up the bonding process. "I'm right here. But Daddy's going to change you."

Bella yelped. Matt just kept going. He walked to the bed and set Bella down.

Claire said, "We should have ordered a changing table."

He peeked back. "What's that?"

"It looks like a chest of drawers for a baby but the top

is made in such a way that you can change her on it. It's higher so changing her is easier."

"Sounds like we should order one when we get back downstairs."

She nodded.

Remembering more of the things he'd seen Claire do, Matt tickled Bella's tummy. "So did you have a good nap?"

She yelped again.

"Not much of a happy riser, are you?"

He unsnapped the crotch of her pajamas, undid her diaper and froze. "Damn."

Standing behind him, her lips pressed together to keep from smiling, Claire only raised her eyebrows when he peeked at her.

"Can you get me a diaper?"

"Yes. I was going to get one before you asked, but decided it was important for you to realize lesson one of diaper changing. Get the clean diaper before you take off the dirty one."

Once again, he had to stifle a laugh. He turned his attention to Bella. "While we wait for the diaper, anything you want to talk about?"

She giggled.

"You know, once you get past that grumpy, first-waking-up stage, you're actually a very happy kid."

Claire handed him the clean diaper. "It's taking less and less time for her to respond to you."

He slid the diaper beneath her and pulled the sides together.

Leaning over his shoulder, Claire said, "You should wipe her bottom with one of these cloths," she offered him a container of baby wipes and he took one. "As you clean her, check to make sure her bottom's not red."

"What do I do if it's red?"

She showed him some creams and ointments in the diaper bag and explained about diaper rash. They pronounced her bottom fine and she took the used wipe from him, tossed it in the trash and turned his attention back to the diaper.

"Attach the strips tighter this time. That prevents accidents, but it's also more comfortable for her not to have her diaper sliding around every time she moves."

He pulled the tabs tighter. "Got it."

Finished, he snapped her sleeper and lifted her from the bed. "Playtime?"

Claire nodded and headed for the door. "First, though, we'll order the changing table." She paused and smiled at him. His heart did the weird thing again, part squeeze, part roll. He loved it when she smiled. But he also knew they were bad for each other and she hadn't meant anything by the smile, except her intention to get along with him while she taught him.

"And a few toys. Things that require a little more of her attention than the bear and the rattles. Things that can actually keep her busy or give you something to do while you play with her."

"Okay."

In only a few minutes on the internet they'd found and ordered the changing table and some interesting toys.

"I like the cone," he said, referring to the toy with the multicolored rings that fit on a cone. "It's simple, but I can see how it will keep her busy."

"And showing her how to play with the rings will give you something to do with her."

Holding Bella, who chewed on her rattle, Matt rose from his seat behind the desk. He didn't get two steps away before his phone rang.

He stopped and Claire stepped forward to get Bella. "I'll take her."

He reached for the phone. "Thanks. I don't get a lot of calls here so this has to be important."

Claire took Bella to the rug in front of the sofa, sat her on the floor and lowered herself beside her. After a few seconds of peekaboo, she crawled to the left of the sofa, hiding from the baby, only to pop out every few seconds and say, "Boo."

There was a voice on the other end of the line, "Mr. Patterson? Are you there?"

Realizing he'd been so preoccupied with Claire that he hadn't even said hello, Matt responded, "Um, sorry. I'm here."

"It's Rafe from Hansen's Department Store. The baby carrier you ordered doesn't come in that shade of pink. We can order one, but we already have it in blue or green."

"I want the pink," he said absently, watching Claire play with Bella. She was a natural with kids and her game reminded him of hot summer days spent at Cedric's beach house, when he and his siblings played hide-and-seek. Though his mother had never joined in, he could see Claire joining her children. He could see her climbing sand mounds at the beach or peeking out from behind trees in the lush yard behind his house. *His* house. *This estate.*

"Also some of the toys will have to be ordered."

He shook his head, bringing himself back to the present. "That's fine."

"Great. We'll deliver what we have in stock this afternoon. And the rest we should have by Thursday."

"Thanks."

But when he hung up the phone, he didn't go over to Bella. Instead, he walked to the front of the desk and sat on the edge. He knew he was supposed to be watching Claire to get the gist of how to play with Bella, but he couldn't stop picturing her with lots of kids. Playing, but always with a mother's eye on them.

And he suddenly realized why he couldn't stop watching her. The picture appealed to him. Her, with kids, and a house that would be a real home. He wouldn't be an interloper being passed off as someone's son. He'd be Daddy.

A squeak erupted from his throat. Now, what was he doing? Trying to make up for his past with a woman he hardly knew…and wanting kids?

That was just wrong.

Bella's giggling brought him back to the present. Claire crawled over to her and tickled her tummy. Then she scooped her up with her as she rose.

"You're such a funny little girl."

Bella squealed with delight.

"You love to play."

She cuddled Bella to her and the baby nestled in. Just about to turn away before he started spinning odd fantasies again, Matt stopped himself.

Maybe he wasn't so much envisioning himself with a family, but Claire. After their discussions today, he'd be an idiot not to realize this was a woman who longed for a family.

He frowned, watching her.

Maybe that's what drew him? They hadn't known each other long enough to really like each other. Yet he couldn't deny being drawn to her. So did he want a family…or did he simply want help with Bella? Real help. Not just a nanny to care for his baby, but someone to love her in ways Matt wasn't sure he could?

CHAPTER NINE

With his new questions about Claire confusing him, Matt spent Wednesday trying to avoid her. But how could he when caring for Bella together put them in the same room all the time? When she finally went to bed, he got a few minutes of peace and quiet, but when he entered his bedroom, he could smell her. Her scent wasn't just in the bathroom anymore. No. It was everywhere.

Thursday morning, Bella seemed to have learned that spitting out her food could be entertaining, so Matt found himself stationed by the high chair, wiping spit food off the tray, putting himself directly in line with Claire's scent.

After breakfast, they rolled a ball back and forth for an hour, keeping Claire's scent around him and emphasizing the fact that they didn't talk.

They couldn't. Every time they talked, they got to know each other. And when he got to know her, he liked her. But when they didn't talk, he thought about her. Wondered how a little girl got along without a mom when she had a distant dad. Wondered why she wasn't bitter, as he was about his family. Wondered how she'd stayed so sweet.

Though he needed to learn everything he could while he had Claire with him, by Thursday afternoon he knew there had to be a better way to handle this. They had to find something to do while they cared for the baby. Something that would occupy their minds enough that he could stop thinking.

He wanted twenty minutes of not thinking. Not about his family, not about Bella and especially not his unwanted attraction to Claire.

He pushed himself away from the desk. "You know what? I think we should spend the rest of the afternoon cooking dinner."

Claire glanced over. "Cooking dinner?"

"Yeah. I'm getting a little tired of takeout. But we also have to spend time with the baby. So I thought we could put her in the high chair and chitchat with her as we put a roast in the oven."

She walked the baby over to him. "That's a great idea. We'll get dinner, but you'll also learn how to multitask with a baby."

"How is that different from regular multitasking?"

"No matter what you're doing, if Bella needs tending to; she becomes the priority. This is a great way to start seeing that."

Matt shook his head, unable to stop the laugh that escaped. "Seriously? You think I'm that stupid?"

He expected her to have some kind of funny comeback. Instead, she froze. "You laughed."

"What you said was either insulting or funny. I chose funny."

"Okay…" She bit her lip. "It's just that—" She stopped again.

"What?"

"When we met you never laughed. You smiled a bit, but sort of craftily like you were trying to figure me out. Then you started 'kind of' laughing. But not really laughing, more like chuckling. You just really laughed. A genuine laugh. As if you're happy."

He headed for the door. "I'm not happy." He stopped, raked his fingers through his hair, as that damned confusion overwhelmed him again. Technically, he was happy. He liked who he was and what he did. "That's not to say I'm unhappy. Things are working out with Bella." He stopped again. What the hell was going on with him? Why did he feel he had to explain himself to her? He strode to the door. "Could we please drop it?"

She raced after him. "Why? I think it's cute. You like Bella. Or maybe you like the idea of being a dad." She smiled dreamily. "It's cute."

He walked out of the office and toward the kitchen. "It's not cute. I'm confused." Realizing he was talking to her again, admitting things he shouldn't, he stopped abruptly and she almost plowed into his back. "Could we just forget it?"

"Okay. Sure. I'm certainly not trying to talk about personal things. But I think Bella makes you happy. That's all I want to say. You don't have to answer, explain or refute it. It's just an observation."

But as they worked together seasoning the roast, peeling potatoes, preparing vegetables to make a salad when the roast was done, she continued to wear that ridiculously dreamy smile. A smile that said she was thrilled all this was working out for Bella.

Bella sat in her high chair, cheerfully banging a rattle on the tray. Claire chopped veggies, dreamily thinking thoughts Matt was absolutely positive he didn't want to know. And he organized everything, getting rid of his pent-up energy and doing what needed to be done. Like the man of the house.

Damn. There he went again. Thinking about things, his

life, in ways that were foreign. He wasn't a family man. He didn't want a family.

But he had one.

And he had to admit that with Bella settling in and him growing accustomed to her he did feel…happy.

All these years he'd thought his successes and toys made had him happy. But the new feeling bubbling through him told him they only made him feel successful.

Claire or Bella or maybe Claire and Bella made him happy.

And it scared the snot out of him.

The buzzer for the gate rang and he walked to the intercom. The screen above the row of buttons showed a truck with the Hansen's Department Store logo on the door.

"Yes."

"I have a delivery for Matt Patterson."

"Gate is opening. Come to the front entrance."

Without looking at Claire, he said, "I'll take care of this," and left the room.

After lighting the burner under the potatoes to cook them for mashed potatoes, Claire fell to the chair near the high chair. "Your daddy is the first person I've ever met who didn't want to be happy."

Bella gurgled.

"You're right. Let's hope he gets accustomed to it." She ruffled Bella's soft tuft of hair. "What am I thinking? *You'll* get him accustomed to it."

She would. Because Bella had the rest of her life to worm her way into his heart.

Which was a very good reminder to Claire. With everything Matt did, she liked him more. Try as he might to be grouchy and sullen, he was growing accustomed to Bella and enjoying being a dad. And that was very attractive. But, though he'd accommodated a baby in his life, this wasn't a guy who would fall head over heels in love with a woman. She'd be lucky if he remembered her name after she left. She wasn't here to make him happy, worm her way into his heart or fall in love. She was here for the baby. And *she'd* do well to remember that.

Claire stayed in the kitchen with Bella and finished the mashed potatoes. When the delivery man left, she unwrapped the additional toys that had arrived that afternoon. She showed Matt how to dump the colored rings from the cone onto the floor and help Bella rearrange them on the cone again. With all the playing, Bella grew tired more quickly than usual and Claire and Matt just barely got her bathed before she fell asleep at seven.

They walked into the kitchen silently. Both of them probably as tired as Bella, and both of them lost in thought.

Matt went directly to the oven. "With her going to bed this early, is she going to sleep tonight?"

Claire shrugged. "Hard to say. But when a baby is falling asleep on your arm, you can't really keep her awake."

He set the roast on the stove. The delicious aroma floated over to Claire and her stomach growled. She set the table as he carved the roast. She got the salad from the refrigerator and put the mashed potatoes into the microwave for a quick reheat.

They sat down to eat as silent as they'd been while putting together their meal.

After a minute of quiet, Matt rose. He pressed a few buttons on the panel containing the intercom and video feed from the gate, and soft music filled the kitchen.

"No reason for us to be completely uncivilized," he said as he returned to his seat.

"Right." She sucked in a breath. Obviously, the quiet in the room got to him, too. But they'd made a promise not to talk about personal things, and neither one of them wanted to risk it. Of course, his job was probably a safe subject.

"Do you do a lot of traveling for your business?"

"Only because I want to. If you're worried about me leaving Bella, I can arrange my schedule so I don't have to." He smiled. "People will come to me."

She nodded, but the urge to tease him rose up in her, so strong and so natural, it nearly stole her breath. Since that kiss, they'd focused on Bella. Hadn't teased. Hadn't meandered into personal territory. And that had worked out very well. No yelling. No hurt feelings. She would not overstep those boundaries.

"Good point."

"So what about you? Have they done okay without you at Dysart Adoptions this week?"

"Easily. Joni and I are basically the only two caseworkers, but with our receptionist we're enough. We go through a lot of slow seasons. We're in one now."

"Me, too." He dug into his mashed potatoes. "I love what I do, though."

"What *exactly* do you do?"

"Buy and sell things. Stocks. Companies."

Comfortable with their safe topic, they talked about his business dealings through the remainder of dinner. She learned he'd gotten his nickname "Iceman" because he could be totally heartless about firing upper management.

Which made her laugh. "Seriously. Who gets all upset about a guy being asked to leave a big corporation when he goes with a golden parachute?"

"You're forgetting who gave me the nickname… Other CEOs. The very people I fire." He frowned. "And we forgot dessert." He glanced over at her. "We don't have dessert."

"You have pudding cups."

"That's right! I do."

He walked to the refrigerator, pulled out two pudding cups and ambled back. "Vanilla or chocolate?"

"Chocolate."

"Great. Vanilla's actually my favorite."

He handed her the pudding cup and took his seat again.

She peeled off the lid, took a bite and groaned in ecstasy. "These are great."

"No point in having a secret vice if it isn't great."

She laughed. "I never thought of that."

They finished their pudding and she automatically got up to clear the table. "You go make your calls or whatever you need to do." The baby monitor had stayed silent. Bella was okay. And she could wash a few dishes.

But he shook his head. "I'm not going to leave you to clean up alone. You're helping me enough."

Warmth spiraled through her. She'd always known he appreciated her help, but it never hurt to hear the words.

After gathering the dishes, she walked them to the sink.

His eyebrows rose. "You're not using the dishwasher?"

"For a couple dishes? We can have these done in five minutes. The dishwasher will take forty and tons more water."

As she filled a sink, he found a dishtowel, slung it over his shoulder, then finished clearing the table.

When the sink was filled to capacity with dirty dishes and sparkling bubbles, she washed a plate, rinsed it and put it in the dish drainer. "Somebody must wash dishes in here. Otherwise, there wouldn't be a drainer."

"I think my cook prefers to wash the pots."

She peeked at him through her peripheral vision. "Really?"

"She's very fussy about her pots."

"Makes sense, I guess. I don't cook much." She glanced at him again. "Not much reason to cook for one."

"Unless you're hungry."

"I eat a big lunch."

"Oh, so in other words if you ever got married and had someone to cook for, you'd start eating supper and get as round as Bella?"

She gaped at him. "Did you just call Bella fat?"

"She's not fat. She's healthy."

Her eyebrow rose. "And I'm not?"

His mouth fell open. "I didn't say that!"

She caught a handful of soap bubbles in her cupped hand and flung them at him. She'd intended to hit his T-shirt. Instead, she got his nose.

The expression on his face was priceless. But shock quickly morphed into challenge. "You wanna go?"

She eeked. "No! You're the one who called me fat."

"I called Bella fat and you unhealthy. According to you." He reached down, scooped out some bubbles and flipped them into her face.

She gasped and, without thought, got more bubbles and flung them at him. "You said what you said."

"You misinterpreted what I said." He grabbed a bigger handful of suds. With a quick twist of his wrist, he got her hair.

"Hey!" Her eyes narrowed. "Don't mess up my hair!"

"You weren't worried about my nose."

"Okay. Fine. If that's how you want it, this is war!"

"Ha! You think you can beat me! I know every corner of this kitchen. And my sister Charlotte and I were very adept at avoiding our other sisters when we were younger." He filled an available cup with water and darted around the table, behind a chair. "Bring it."

"You wouldn't throw an entire cup of water at me!"

"Guess again."

"And who's going to clean up the mess?"

He shrugged. "Us. When we're done with our war."

Her face contorted. "Why throw the water when you end up having to clean it up?"

"For the fun of the war." He walked from behind the table. "You really didn't have much of a childhood."

She shrugged. "Looks like I didn't."

"Great." He dribbled some water on her head.

Expecting his sympathy and getting a shower, she jumped back sputtering. "What are you doing!"

"We're at war, remember? If I were you, I'd get a cup."

Her eyes narrowed, but he only grinned. Knowing he wouldn't stay passive long, she raced to the sink and got a cup of water, but she paused. "This is ridiculous."

She watched his face sort of deflate. Cup in hand, he walked to the sink, clearly disappointed that he'd failed in getting her to play. When he was close enough, she sloshed the water out of her cup and onto his shirt.

He gasped and jumped back. "You tricked me."

She refilled her cup and scampered away. "All is fair in love and war."

"Oh, this is so on."

She ran to the kitchen island, shielding herself behind it and the rows of pots that hung above it.

"You have to come out sometime."

"Not really. I think I can safely protect myself behind this island for the rest of the war."

She bounced out for one quick slosh toward him, the way an Old West gunfighter bounces from behind a tree just long enough to shoot, then was back behind her island again.

He bent away from the spray. "You missed me."

"I'll get you next time."

He nudged his chin in the direction of her cup. "Not without water." He glanced around. "Let's see. I have a whole cup of water and I stand between you and the sink." He smiled evilly. "Who's winning now?"

She said, "Eek!" and dodged to the right.

When she got to the open space in the overhead pots, he flung his water at her and got her on the chest, soaking her T-shirt.

She glanced down at it in amazement. Then up at him. Then burst out laughing. "All right. One of us has to call a truce."

He walked to the sink. Refilled his cup. Displayed it for her to see. "Or one of us has to surrender."

"Okay. Now you're just being childish."

"And throwing cups of water wasn't? We're just having fun…and I think you're trying to talk your way out of losing the war."

"I'm trying to talk us back to adulthood."

"Why?" He glanced around. "No one's here. No one cares."

But she cared. When he behaved like a silly, fun guy, strange feelings of warmth and happiness danced through her. And fantasies began to spin in her head. She'd never wanted a stuffy, formal family. She wanted a happy family. With a happy dad. And right now he was behaving as if he could be one.

But he couldn't. He was Wall Street's Iceman. This little thing they were doing with the water had to be an aberration.

She raised her hands in surrender. "All right. I surrender."

A look of disappointment flitted across his face, but he didn't put his cup down. Like the town sheriff arresting the bad guy, he brandished it like a gun. "Walk your cup to the sink."

She laughed. "This is ridiculous."

"No, this is how a smart man ends a war, especially when his opponent has already duped him once."

She giggled. "Really? Seriously? I have to walk my cup to the sink."

"And dump out the contents."

As she ambled to the sink, he edged around, so he could see her every move.

She laughed again.

"Now dump it out."

She poured the remaining water from her cup into the empty sink.

"And put the cup into the dishwater in the other sink."

Pressing her lips together to stop another giggle, she put the cup in the water.

"Now step away from the sink."

"You really get into this role playing, don't you?"

"Charlotte and I rarely lost a water battle."

"Sounds like your childhood was fun."

He said, "It was. But I'm still watching you. Put both hands up and step away from the sink."

This time she let the gale of laughter roll out of her. She walked far enough away from the sink to appease him. "That was fun. That was *really* fun."

Watching her warily, he set his cup on the sink. "Yeah, it was."

She glanced down at herself. "Except I'm soaked."

Following the line of her vision, he saw that her sodden T-shirt had molded to her, outlining her perfect breasts. The wonderful feeling of joy enveloping them suddenly shifted. It was clear she'd never had an ounce of fun as a kid and something inside him wanted to show her all of that. Show her how to have fun.

Him. The Iceman. He wanted to show somebody how to have fun.

He hadn't thought about fun in twenty years.

Yet she made him want to have fun again.

And if that wasn't confusing enough, looking at her, dripping wet and incredibly sexy, his definition of fun had morphed from water battles to adult games in his amazing shower. He wanted to make love but not in a serious, purely physical way. In a fun, joyful way.

He stepped back, cleared his throat. "You are wet. Why don't you go upstairs first and get a shower? I'll be up in a minute."

She smiled like a happy child. "Yeah. Guess I should."

She turned without another thought for the dishes or cleaning up the water they'd tossed at each other. But as Matt grabbed a mop—from a closet he found after searching around awhile—he told himself he didn't mind cleaning up after their water battle.

He needed to be away from her for a few minutes. Not only had she awakened urges in him he hadn't felt... well, ever. But also, water fighting with her reminded him of happier times. Magnificently simple times when he'd thought his sisters were his sisters. When there were no half anythings. And everybody loved a good water battle in the pool, the ocean or the bathroom.

He grinned stupidly. They were bad kids, but he'd loved that part of his childhood.

His grin faded. He missed his sisters. Not the adult versions, but the kids he used to play with.

A great ache filled his chest.

He missed being happy.

But when he finished cleaning the kitchen he went to

his room and absently ambled into the bathroom; he forgot he had a guest. He found Claire brushing her teeth in front of one of the bowls of his double-bowl sinks and his thoughts swung back in the other direction.

In her pretty pink pajamas, with her little pink toes sticking out and her big brown eyes still shining with laughter, she was the epitome of that perfect mom he'd suspected she'd be. Happy. Filled with joy. Waiting for her husband to come to bed. So they could—

He jumped back. Not out of embarrassment that he'd walked in on her in the bathroom. But because that vision scared him. After Ginny, he always pictured himself alone—believed he deserved to be alone. Now in a few days one little slip of a woman had him thinking about family, kids, fun…and sex filled with emotion. Not just physical pleasure, but physical pleasure wrapped in a blanket of happiness.

This woman scared him.

"I'll just go back out and wait until you're finished."

She spit in the sink. That alone should have had him running. Instead, it felt very natural, very normal.

"No. No. I'm just about done. You can come in."

He hesitated, then walked in. This was ridiculous. How could one person change what you felt about everything? In four days? From Monday to Thursday? And could he really count Monday, since he hadn't gotten to Dysart Adoptions until after four? It was ridiculous.

He ambled to the sink, got his toothbrush and rolled some paste on it.

Towel-drying her hair, she said, "So tomorrow, we interview nannies."

He nodded.

"That should be easy. Especially after the water battle."

She caught his gaze in the mirror and smiled at him.

"Now, we both know you're looking for someone fun. Someone who can play with Bella."

Yeah, *her.* He was looking for her. She might not have played games as a child, but she knew how to play with Bella and she'd happily played with him. She longed to play. And he longed to teach her to play. To be happy. To be part of a family.

His eyes locked on hers in the mirror. He felt a thousand longings spring up, a thousand possibilities and a thousand things he never in a million years believed he'd feel.

It was everything he could do not to run out of the bathroom.

CHAPTER TEN

THE next morning, Matt barely looked at Claire when they woke up with Bella. He silently changed the baby's diaper and carried her downstairs.

Claire's heart stuttered a bit. She'd fallen asleep foolishly happy. They'd had fun in the water battle. And she'd seen that playful, wonderful side of him again. Having him withdraw stung, even if it did remind her to watch herself. She wasn't supposed to like him too much. He was wrong for her. The bits and pieces of Happy Matt that she saw came and went. They were too fleeting to be dependable. And he didn't want her, either. Otherwise, he'd have been happy this morning. Flirty as he was the night before. Not sullen, as if he regretted everything they'd done.

She prepared Bella's cereal and, again, Matt insisted he be the one to feed her.

She gave him the spoon and sat on the chair across the table from them.

"Here you are, sweetie," he crooned, sliding the bite of cereal into the baby's mouth. Bella smiled sleepily before opening her mouth wide to take it.

Matt laughed. "You make this easy, Miss Bella."

Claire smiled, too. It might not be wise for her to get involved with him, but when he wasn't being Wall Street's

Iceman, he was definitely nicer than he believed himself to be.

She frowned. This was another thing Ginny had probably seen while married to him. Buried deep down inside of Matt there really was a nice guy.

But if he was always working, how could Ginny have seen that? When had she seen nice Matt? When they met? Had they gone to school together?

"How'd you meet Bella's mom?"

Preoccupied with feeding Bella, Matt said, "We took the same train to work."

She frowned. That didn't give Ginny much chance to see him as a nice guy. "Really? You rode a train?"

"Subway. I lived in New York City back then."

"It's still hard to see you on a train."

"I told you. I learned all about good money management while attending university. Just because I'd gotten a great job, I wasn't about to throw my money lessons out the window. I lived conservatively and was never poor again."

"So how'd you meet? Did you sit beside each other?"

He smiled. "Actually, I'd noticed her on the train for weeks before we spoke. It wasn't until I gave a pregnant woman my seat and ended up standing beside her that I talked to her."

His smile grew. "She was beautiful. Every guy in the train had talked to her, but she'd blown them off." He turned and met Claire's gaze briefly. "Until we suddenly found ourselves holding the same pole. Then I said something goofy and she laughed. After that, we sat beside each other every day. Saved each other seats." He paused, his head tilted. "We talked. A lot. Before I could screw up the courage to ask her out."

He peeked over his shoulder at her again. "You could make coffee."

"Good idea." She rose from the chair and walked to the counter. But considering everything he'd just told her—how he and Ginny had met, how they'd stayed friends even after their divorce and how Ginny had given Bella to Matt to raise, she spun around again.

Ginny hadn't given him a second look until he relinquished his seat to a pregnant woman. Then she'd talked to him. And it wasn't until they'd talked several times—on their train rides—that she'd gone out with him. She hadn't just believed Matt to be a nice guy. She'd tested him. She'd seen him do a good deed, then quizzed him. That's why she'd believed him to be honorable and good, and strong enough to raise her child. She'd gotten to know the real Matt before she even agreed to go out with him.

And that was why Claire kept falling for him. Just like Ginny, she'd been given a space of time to see the real Matt Patterson. Had they met any other way she'd have met the Iceman. Cool. Calculating. Watching him with Bella, she was getting to know his good side.

No. That wasn't true, either. It was more like being stuck together for days, twenty-four hours each day, they were getting to know the real people they were underneath.

And underneath all his bluster, Matt Patterson was a genuinely nice guy.

After the coffee brewed, she poured two cups and walked back to the table.

Claire set his coffee in front of him. "Our first nanny interview isn't until nine. We can take a few minutes, drink our coffee and chat with her."

Matt took a sip from his coffee, then glanced at Bella. "So what do you want to talk about today?"

Bella giggled.

But strange thoughts went through Claire's brain. He was getting so good with Bella. Not merely competent. But loving. Treating her as his own child. Making the two of them a family without even realizing it.

She didn't know why she was surprised. She'd seen hints, even before Monday was over, that he had what it took to be a great dad.

The question was…

Did he have what it took to be a great husband?

And did she have what it took to hang around long enough for him to realize they belonged together?

The thought made her freeze in place. When had she decided they belonged together?

She thought about the night before, having fun, talking normally, just genuinely liking each other, and she realized she and Happy Matt were incredibly compatible. That was the guy she liked. The guy she might even be falling in love with. The guy she could easily see herself spending the rest of her life with.

Iceman Matt was another story. And Iceman Matt seemed to be around more often than not.

Still… What she wouldn't give for a chance, a real chance, to be with Happy Matt.

Maybe if she just continued to make him laugh, to treat him normally, as if life was supposed to be fun, he'd come out and stay out.

The first nanny arrived at nine and Matt led her to the den. She took a seat in front of his desk and Claire sat on the chair beside her.

"So…" He glanced at her résumé, then quickly looked up at her. "Peaches?"

"Yes. My mother apparently had terrible cravings when

she was pregnant with me." She pointed at her head. "The red hair was just a happy accident."

He laughed. Then caught himself. He could count on one hand the times he generally laughed in one week, but lately everything seemed to strike him as funny.

He knew why. Claire was bringing emotions out in him that he'd repressed for years. But he'd repressed them for good reason. He didn't get along with his family. He didn't make a good husband. So, it hurt him to miss his sisters. It hurt to see himself as a family man—when he knew he wasn't a family man. He was a strong, determined businessman who would literally have to squeeze a baby into his life. He had to get himself back to normal. And the best way to get himself back to normal would be to hire a nanny and get Claire out of his house.

Though the thought of her leaving hurt, too, that was actually the point. She made him want things he couldn't have. And he would feel these odd things until she left. But once she was gone, he'd be fine.

He looked at Peaches's résumé again. He asked her a few questions about her employment, but no matter how hard he tried to poke holes in her experience he couldn't. Peaches—however odd her name—was a candidate for Bella's nanny.

He ushered her to the front door, and when he returned to the den, Claire grinned at him. A responding grin rose up in him but he squelched it.

"I liked her."

He walked to his desk. "I did, too. But I have to admit, I was hoping for someone more conservative."

She laughed. "Conservative? After our water battle?"

His gaze dipped to the desk. "That water battle was stupid."

"That water battle was fun."

He knew it was. But the crazy urges it brought out in

him were wrong. He'd spent the past twelve years on his own, even when he was married to Ginny, becoming successful by keeping his nose to the grindstone. That's who he was. He needed to remember that.

"Oh, surely you're not regretting our water battle?"

Thoughts of sloshing water on her made him want to laugh again and brought his longings to life. He shouldn't want to be playful and silly. But more important, he didn't have the right to risk Claire's heart by dragging her into fantasies that had no place for him. Fantasies that would dissolve like dust as soon as he got back to work. If he didn't settle this right now, she'd get her hopes up and they'd have a real mess on their hands.

"Actually, I am."

"But—"

"No buts. I'm a single man with a conglomerate that takes most, if not all, of my time, trying to fit a baby into my life. I should be taking this more seriously."

"I think you're doing exactly—"

"Stop! I know you think I need to change and I know you're leading me in that direction. But I am who I am. I promise you I will raise Bella well. You can stop worrying and stop trying to change me."

She pressed her lips together as if he'd mortally embarrassed her and Matt's heart compressed into a tiny ball. Or maybe it went back to the shape it always had been—a tiny, tiny ball.

A tiny ball that would barely be able to handle loving a baby let alone adding a sweet, wonderful woman to the list.

The doorbell rang. She bounced out of her seat. "I'll bring this nanny back."

Pretending great interest in the résumé for the next nanny, he let her go.

* * *

The remainder of the interviews went smoothly. They chose three great candidates, any one of whom would make a great nanny, and Matt was suddenly extremely happy.

But Claire knew why. Once he got a nanny, she would leave. No wonder his mood had lifted. No more being pushed about Bella or how he should behave or what he should do.

Well, okay. She got the message. He did not want to be pushed into being the guy she got along with, the guy she liked.

She swallowed down the sadness that filled her. Not just for herself but for him. She wasn't a stranger to loneliness and she recognized all the signs in Matt. But he didn't want her help. And she—

Well, she was tired of being rejected. After their water battle she'd thought something had changed between them, but Matt regretted it. He regretted laughing with her. He regretted having fun with her.

And she was really tired of being someone's regret. First her dad's. Then Ben's. Now Matt's?

She didn't think so.

It was time to distance herself. Really distance herself. Tomorrow he would conduct second interviews. By tomorrow night he could have a nanny and she could go home. Protect her heart. Never be somebody's regret again.

But as she turned to leave the room, regret rose up in *her*. Regret that she hadn't been able to reach him, to make him want her enough to forget all the things that tied him down. All the reasons he wanted to stay lonely.

When Bella woke from her nap, Claire lifted her from her crib and immediately handed her to Matt. When the baby wouldn't settle, Claire drifted away, hoping that being out of sight would put her out of the baby's mind.

No such luck.

Matt might not be a total stranger to her, but fresh from a nap when Bella was disoriented and in need of the familiar, Matt wasn't the person she wanted to hug.

Finally, she walked over, took Bella from Matt and said, "She needs her things."

"Whatever she wants we can buy."

"No. I didn't say that she *wanted* her things. I said she *needs* her things. *Her* things." If her voice was a little snippy, she didn't care. This baby needed some comfort. And it seemed they were always catering to Matt. What he wanted. How he wanted things done. That stopped here. That stopped now. "She needs the things that make her relax. Things that make her happy. We need to go to her house, get her special stuffed animal, see if she had a particular blanket she slept with, find her favorite snuggly pajamas."

"She'll get accustomed to—"

"Hey!" Her temper boiled over. She was coming to like a guy who obviously didn't want to like her, while caring for a baby she was going to miss. She needed to get this job done and get away before she got any more emotionally involved. The time for diplomacy had passed. "In almost four days she hasn't grown accustomed to you. Why the hell should she suddenly fall in love with a strange bear?"

Matt's eyebrows rose.

Claire stiffened. That had been stupid. She never, ever vented like that. But he had her so frustrated. The whole situation did. Why was she upset over losing a man she barely knew? Especially one who was now sorry they'd had a water battle that had made her laugh like nothing in her entire life had ever made her laugh. They'd had so much fun and now he regretted it.

Why did he want to be a grouchy man when he had such a wonderful man inside him?

She headed for the nursery door. "Come with me or stay behind. But Bella and I are going to her former house to get the things that will make her comfortable."

As she left the room, she heard Matt's annoyed breath, but by the time she got Bella into a little jacket and found her own coat, he was behind her, walking toward the limo with her.

Realizing she hadn't called Jimmy, she stopped.

He nudged her to keep going. "I called him."

It didn't amaze her that it seemed he'd read her mind. He hadn't. He'd thought of Jimmy because when he needed to go somewhere he always called Jimmy. She refused to make a big deal out of him knowing what she was thinking. This whole situation was a mess. A setup for disaster. Them playing house. Her already in love with Bella and falling for the nice guy Matt showed her when he let his guard down. Him being sweet one minute, grouchy the next.

What woman wouldn't be confused?

They drove to a beautiful estate not far from Matt's and also not as big or elaborate. About half the size of Matt's, the two-story brick house sat on a green lawn.

He unbuckled Bella, told Jimmy they'd only be about ten minutes and led her up the walk.

She glanced around with a gasp. "I never thought about security. How are we going to get in?"

He pulled a key from his pocket. "We're covered."

Of course, if Ginny trusted him enough to give him her baby, she'd certainly trust him with a key to her house.

After punching numbers into a pad by the door, he used the key and let them inside.

Silent and eerie, the front hall greeted them. Walking into the home of people she didn't know—especially considering those two people were dead—filled her with trepidation. But when Bella squealed with delight, sadness quickly replaced Claire's fears. Sorrow seeped into her soul. This was Bella's home. The last time she'd been here she'd been with her mommy and daddy.

Matt, however, didn't pause. He walked up the curving stairway, led Claire to a room in the back and opened the door on a nursery.

Claire whispered. "How did you know where it was?"

"I am her godfather. It was mandatory that I peek in on her occasionally."

"You make it sound like you'd only looked at her as a favor to her parents."

He cocked his head. "I guess that *was* all I did it for."

Disappointed in him, she said, "Oh," and followed him into the nursery. A well-worn pink blanket lay in the crib. As soon as she saw it, Bella screeched.

Claire scooped it up and Bella grabbed it. Pressing her face into the soft material, she cooed with delight.

"I think we've found her blanket."

Matt stood off to the side, stiff, erect. "What else does she need?"

Claire looked around. "Let's let her decide." She smiled at Bella. "What else, sweetie?"

Blanket over her arm, Bella stretched toward the crib again. Claire walked over and saw the big-eared stuffed dog. She pulled it out.

Bella squawked, hugging the dog like a lifeline.

"Two things down. I don't know how many more to go."

"How many does she need? Seriously. We've got her dog and her blanket. Isn't that enough?"

Hearing the annoyance in his voice, Claire nearly turned on him again. If this was the Iceman, she was glad he hadn't put in too many appearances. "I don't know. We should probably get some of her clothes. Especially pajamas. Then we can go."

"Great." He walked to her. "I'll hold Bella. You pack a bag for her."

Claire found a big diaper bag and as quickly as she could she filled it with baby clothes. Not the beautiful, obviously expensive things she found in the closet, though she chose a few of those. What she was most interested in were the worn jeans, scruffy pajamas, soft T-shirts. The things she suspected Bella probably wore all the time. The things that would make Bella comfortable.

Without her.

She was being replaced by worn pajamas, a soft blanket and a big-eared scruffy dog.

Her eyes filled with tears, but anger soon dried them. All Matt would have to do would be to say one word and she would visit Bella. Regularly. But no. He didn't want to play. He didn't want to be soft. He wouldn't trust. And she wouldn't put herself out there only to be rejected again.

When the diaper bag was full, she walked to the door. Matt followed silently behind her.

But at the bottom of the stairs, he stopped. He sucked in a breath and squeezed his eyes shut.

"What?"

He swallowed. "This was the house Ginny and I had lived in. I gave it to her in the divorce. She liked it enough that she kept it."

Damn.

Remorse for all her nasty thoughts about his mood filled her. Not sure what to say, she stayed silent.

He shook his head. "We really did have a happy beginning to our marriage."

"Most beginnings are happy."

"And then work got in the way."

At the sadness in his voice, pain pierced her heart. He and Ginny might have divorced but they'd obviously loved each other.

She glanced around, suddenly understanding something else about Matt Patterson. He wasn't just struggling with the idea of his life changing drastically because of getting Bella after Ginny's death. He'd lost a woman he'd once loved and he was grieving. "You really loved her."

He peeked over at her, as if reluctant to admit any more personal things to her. But finally he said, "Yes. But the deals always took me away."

"You were trying to prove yourself to your stepfather."

He barked a laugh. "If nothing else, I know you pay attention when I talk."

Had that been an insult or a compliment? "Am I wrong?"

He shifted Bella on his arm. "No. You're not wrong. My need to prove myself was stronger than my need to keep her." He paused, swallowed. "The thing is, I always believed she'd stay. I believed if she loved me she'd want what I wanted."

"But she didn't."

"No."

An odd sensation enveloped her. As if she understood the sadness Ginny had felt when she'd divorced him. The disappointment that she'd lost the man she'd married, the man she'd loved.

Still, she said nothing. She felt for Matt, but she also

understood Ginny. She'd barely come up on her father's radar because of his work. It would be a hundred times sadder to lose the man you adored, the man you knew still lived somewhere deep down inside your husband.

She hoisted the diaper bag to her shoulder. "Let's go."

"Okay." He followed her to the front door. But before stepping out, he took one final survey of the front foyer.

Her heart broke for him, but she couldn't say anything comforting or soothing. He didn't want her to, but she also knew this was something he'd have to come to terms with himself.

There were no words of comfort for someone who was guilty as charged.

CHAPTER ELEVEN

CLAIRE tossed the diaper bag into the car and slid in. Matt climbed in and strapped Bella into the car seat. As Jimmy started the limo, Matt leaned back. Seeing Ginny's house, seeing how Bella had reacted to her blanket and well-worn dog, he'd figured out some things. Ginny had turned the house they'd lived in into a home. A real home. Even without people, it hadn't seemed empty.

From the second he'd walked in the door, he'd seen signs of her and Oswald everywhere. A pipe in an ashtray. Vacation pictures. Comfortable sofas in the living room beside the foyer. Throw rugs to catch dirt from shoes. Colorful afghans on chairs for chilly winter nights. People lived in that house and it showed.

While his house was big and cold and certainly not kid-friendly.

Most of that he could fix with a remodel. But he couldn't change the fact that his house was sterile, unless he brought more people into his life. His first thought was Claire. She'd be the perfect mother for Bella. She'd brighten the house more than any remodel possibly could. And he wanted her. He'd sleep with her in a heartbeat and she'd sleep with him. He knew she had feelings for him. Strong feelings. She couldn't keep them out of her eyes, her voice. She wasn't just attracted to him. She liked him.

But she wanted a real home, not the shell she'd have with a man too repressed to feel emotions. Forget about expressing them.

Driving away from the house he'd shared with the last woman he'd hurt, he knew he couldn't draw Claire into a relationship. It wouldn't be fair.

Which took him to his family.

Since the water battle with Claire, he'd been thinking about his sisters. Charlotte was now married and had a child. *A baby.* Maybe having another baby around was what Bella needed?

His heart lifted. Charlotte was the closest of his siblings. He could see Bella playing with her baby. But Charlotte lived in Italy now. Though her visits would be special, they would be few and far between. He needed more. Bella needed more. People to come and go. People who populated pictures on his mantel, pictures he'd take at picnics and on vacations with aunts, uncles, cousins.

A family.

He needed to make more of an effort with his sisters. He'd been cold. He'd been distant. Because he'd been hurt by Cedric. But punishing his sisters for things Cedric had said had been wrong. Plus, Cedric was sick now. It was time to let go of the past.

Still, he needed to vet this with someone. See if it really was the good idea he thought it was. And Claire, like always, was available. "I've been thinking a lot about my family."

Claire faced him, but her voice was cool when she said, "Because of the reunion?"

"And Bella." He cautiously caught her gaze. "And the water fight. I know this is going to sound weird, but I miss my sisters as kids. I'd like to bring them back into my life so Bella would have family. A big family. Lots of family."

"That sounds very nice."

He put his head back. "Problem is I don't know them as adults. I was the oldest. I left for school at eighteen. Didn't even visit. I told my mom I needed my weekends and holidays to work." He peeked over at her. "And that wasn't a lie. I did need to work."

"But you actually stayed away because you were angry with your stepdad?"

"And I took it out on everybody."

"So you've barely seen them."

He nodded. "I've attended a function here and there. But that's it."

"So maybe this reunion would be a great chance to catch up?"

"It would." He reached over and ran his finger across the tiny hand Bella had resting on the bumper pad that kept her in the car seat. She caught it and cooed. "I want Bella to have family."

"That's really good!"

He frowned. He knew that news would make her happy. But after her being nothing but cool in this conversation, her overly bright response was out of place. It was as if she'd noticed he hadn't included her in the equation. If it hurt her, she wouldn't show it. But by not arguing or asking why she wasn't included, it also proved she accepted it. He was shoving her out of his life because that's what he always did. He wouldn't commit to another woman. The visit to Ginny's house should have shown her why she should be glad to get away while she could.

When they reached his house, she quickly undid Bella and carried her inside. Walking up the stairway, she told him she didn't want his help putting the baby to bed.

He wasn't surprised. She was cutting ties. The way

they should be. So he didn't press to join her and Bella in the nursery. He walked back to the den.

Even before he reached his desk, the phone rang.

"Matt Patterson."

"Hey, big brother!"

"Charlotte?"

"Yep. Look, I know you're going to hate this, but I promised I'd call you and tell you so I'm just going to spit it out."

Fearing the worst, he fell to his chair. "So spit."

"Holt's called a family meeting for tomorrow. He wants us all on the same page before the Larkville festivities start next Wednesday."

Holt. The man who would be the family patriarch had Matt not been born a few months earlier. His first reaction was to want to dig in his heels and refuse to come. But after his thoughts that day, he sat back on his seat, considered a different path.

"Will Alex and Ellie be there?" he asked, referring to his and Charlotte's other two sisters.

"They're already here."

He squeezed his eyes shut. It was now or never. Swallow his pride and do what had to be done, or worry that Bella would grow up alone, as isolated as he was. He glanced around his quiet, quiet den. Even knowing Claire and Bella were upstairs, the house was hollow, empty. Missing something that could only be filled by people. Family.

He blew out his breath. "Okay, count me in. I can't be there until afternoon, but I'll be there."

He heard the surprise in her voice as she said, "Family meeting's at six. Let me know when you arrive and I'll pick you up at the airstrip."

He hung up the phone with butterflies in his stomach.

He didn't know how he was supposed to blend into this family, when technically he should be the leader. But if he demanded his place as leader, he'd undoubtedly alienate everyone.

Sighing, he rose from his chair. He'd figure something out.

Upstairs with Bella, Claire couldn't shake a huge case of guilt. After the cool way she'd treated Matt at Ginny's, and the even cooler way she'd reacted when he tried to talk to her about his family, it just didn't feel right to be leaving the next day. Yes, there was no defense for his ignoring Ginny in favor of proving himself to his stepdad, but she could have said something consoling. Maybe even said that the way he worked to become a real father to Bella proved he wasn't the same guy who'd constantly deserted Ginny. He was changing.

But that was the whole point, wasn't it? He was changing. Slowly. But still, he was changing. And when he'd finally talked about Ginny, she'd given him the cold shoulder, wouldn't console him. She'd let him stew.

When he'd most needed her, she'd emotionally deserted him.

She rocked Bella on the rocker, let her snuggle with her dog and blanket and listened to the happy baby murmurs of a little girl finally reunited with a few things that brought her comfort. Though one kind of peace settled over her, it only shined a light on how uneasy she felt about Matt.

It had been so wrong not to comfort him, but he'd told her to butt out of his life. So she had. She had for her own self-protection as much as to comply with his order. She already worried that she was falling in love with him.

And he didn't want to reciprocate those feelings. She'd be crazy to think otherwise.

Still…he needed her. She knew he needed her. Getting back with his family, making amends, wouldn't be easy. He'd need somebody in his corner.

And this time tomorrow she'd be gone.

Matt called the nanny service and canceled the interviews scheduled for the following day. Then he talked to his pilot and called Charlotte back with an arrival time. As he hung up the phone from talking to his sister, Claire walked into the room.

"How's Bella?"

"Sleeping like an angel, happily hugging her blanket and dog."

Finally, finally, things were working out. Now he just had to tell Claire that as of tomorrow, at about noon, her services would no longer be required.

His heart squeezed at that, but he ignored it. She deserved a good man. He was not a good man. The fun they'd had in the water battle was an aberration. Being so comfortable in his bathroom, a mistake. He needed to let her go.

"Would you mind taking a seat?"

She hesitated, then pasted on a smile. He could tell she knew what was coming. Even if he hadn't decided to go to Larkville, she would have been able to go home tomorrow after the nanny came on the job. A smart woman, she would understand it was time to discuss her leaving.

"I just got a call from my sister. It seems my half brother Holt has called a family meeting for tomorrow."

"A family meeting?"

"Our Calhoun/Patterson reunion is tied up with a community festival. They'll be honoring my biological father at a big party next Saturday."

"Oh."

"I don't know Holt, but if he's smart he's probably getting us all there early to give us time to talk through the fact that the man being honored actually has twins he didn't know."

She frowned.

"Ellie and I were conceived in my mother and Clay's very short marriage. He never knew about us because his soon-to-be new wife hid the letter my mother sent informing him of her pregnancy."

Her eyes widened. "You're a twin?"

He almost smiled. She didn't bat an eye at the scandal surrounding Clay Calhoun never knowing his kids. But she was agog over the fact that he was a twin. "Yes. My sister's name is Ellie."

She gaped at him. "How can you have a twin and not talk about her?"

"I told you. I haven't really spoken to most of my family in a decade. But that's over now and I've decided to go to the family meeting. Which means I leave tomorrow."

"Well, I guess that's great. You know…for your family and all."

"It is and it isn't. Because I'm leaving early, I had to cancel the nanny interviews.…"

She frowned. "So who'll be staying with Bella?"

"I'm taking her with me."

"By yourself?"

He'd planned on getting help from his sisters once they were in Texas but he'd forgotten about the plane ride itself. And from the expression on Claire's face he guessed it wasn't a good idea for him to travel with a baby alone.

Before he could say anything, she looked away.

He didn't blame her. After the distant way he'd behaved since their discussion of the water battle, she wasn't going to volunteer. But, of course, after the way he'd behaved, asking her to accompany him now would not be construed as anything other than the favor it would be. So maybe it was a blessing they'd had their spat?

"I know it's an imposition to ask, but could you come with us?"

She said nothing.

"I wouldn't ask, but it's important for me to go to that meeting tomorrow." He leaned back in his chair. "Technically, I'm the oldest. Holt's the oldest of his family, but I'm our father's first son. I should be family patriarch."

Her gaze snapped to his. "You're not going down there to start a fight, are you?"

He laughed. "No, I am not going down there to fight."

"Then why is it suddenly so important?"

"I told you. Not only is Holt apparently staving off potentially embarrassing scenes, but also I came to some conclusions today. I want Bella to have a family. I'm willing to do more than compromise."

She studied him. "Really?"

He sucked in a breath. "Yeah. I just don't know yet what I'm going to do or how I'm going to do it, but I want at least my sisters in Bella's life. If I have to swallow my pride to do it, I will."

Laughing, she shook her head. "Well, I'll be damned."

"Don't make fun. This isn't going to be easy for me."

Slowly, she brought her gaze to meet his. "It might not be easy but it's the right thing. I'm not making fun of you. I'm proud of you."

Warmth spiraled through him at her praise. The truth was he was a tad proud of himself for being willing to make the first moves to get his family back. And not for himself. For Bella. In the past few days he'd done all kinds of good things. He'd been changing with leaps and bounds, genuinely understanding the right things for Bella, and he had Claire to thank for that.

He cleared his throat. Now was not the time to be thinking good thoughts about Claire. He'd finally resolved their situation in his mind. He didn't want those strange feelings he had for her bubbling up again, confusing things. Especially since he needed her again.

Before he could say anything, she did. "I'll go with you."

"You will?"

"Yes. You're going to make a good daddy, Matt Patterson. And if my spending a few more days with you and Bella helps that along, then I'll go to Texas." She laughed and rose from her seat. "I better do some laundry, get my jeans and shirts washed since that's all the clothes I have."

She left the room and Matt stared after her. No ranting or raving about clothes. No telling him what *she* needed. She was doing this only for Bella and him. Getting nothing out of it for herself. Yet, she just left the room to do some laundry as if favors were an everyday occurrence for her.

She was definitely too good for him.

The next morning, Claire called Joni.

"We're taking the baby to Texas."

"And you're calling because you don't think you'll be back on Monday?"

"I have no idea when we'll get back." She winced. "Matt actually talked about a banquet next Saturday night. I'm going to need another week off."

"Okay. As your boss, I'm fine with another week off.

As you're friend, my reaction is… What the hell are you thinking?"

She laughed. "He took everything to another level yesterday. He isn't just determined to be a good dad for Bella. He's also reuniting with his family. He hasn't really been involved in his family in years and, because of Bella, he's taking steps to be in their lives again."

"Seriously? Claire. This is not your problem. There's always going to be one more thing with this guy and before you know it you're going to have been his temporary nanny for a year…or two…with no pay!"

"I'm helping a friend." She paused, wincing, knowing how bad this sounded, but convinced she was doing the right thing. "Matt's a good guy. Bella's a sweet baby. None of this has been easy for him, but I know my being around has helped him and I can't desert him now."

She didn't mention that she'd left him to flounder on the trip to Ginny's house and still felt bad about that. She didn't mention the funny catch in her heart when she thought about how hard he'd worked and how far he'd come. She also didn't mention that she worried that she was falling in love with him, because that didn't count. She knew the compromises he was making for Bella and his family were difficult enough. There wasn't any room in his head or his heart for a romance. No matter how much she liked him or how much she wanted it, he didn't. She *would* remember that.

"And I promise, once we get back from Texas, that will be it. I will walk away."

"I hope so."

"I will."

She disconnected the call and fed Bella some cereal. A few minutes later, Matt stumbled into the kitchen. Wearing his navy striped pajamas without a robe, he looked sleepy and sexy and, oh, so huggable.

She wanted to swoon, but didn't. If she was going to behave as she'd told Joni she would, and keep her heart intact, then this was a business trip for her. She might see a good side of him. She might desperately want to help him. She might even be more attracted to him than she'd ever been to another man, but he'd warned her off several times. She would handle this trip like a professional.

"What time are we leaving for Texas?"

"What time do you want to go?"

"Well, I washed my jeans and my few tops last night, so I'm as ready as I'll ever be."

He turned. "You don't want to go home and get more clothes?"

She shrugged. Unable to think of anything she'd like to take with her, she said, "I have no idea what the weather will be like or how the locals will dress. I'd like to wait and see what everyone else wears. Then I can pick up a few things while I'm there."

He said, "Okay," and faced the coffeepot again.

He played with Bella as he drank his coffee, cementing her belief that he was a nice guy who deserved her help.

While he packed a bag for himself, she packed a bag for Bella. Jimmy drove them to the airport.

When she saw Matt's plane, her eyebrows rose in surprise. "It's kinda small."

"I have no need for a bigger plane."

"Just thought you'd want to be a little fancy."

Carrying Bella, while Jimmy handed their luggage to the eager flight crew, Matt said, "Wait until you see the inside."

The inside was white leather. Soft-cushioned seats that looked like recliners greeted them. He showed her a big-screen TV along a back wall that they could watch in-flight because their seats completely turned around.

The plane taxied and was airborne in a few minutes. Bella fell asleep immediately and Matt showed Claire how to work the TV before he pulled some papers from a brief-case. A comfortable silence settled over them.

She smiled and relaxed against the seat, pleased that everything was calm and content. She had nothing to worry about. They were friends.

A tug on her heart reminded her that she wanted to be more than friends, but she ignored it.

He didn't want her. She wouldn't want him.

When they landed at the small airstrip in front of a hangar at the back of the ranch, Matt unbuckled his seat belt and immediately reached for the one securing Bella's safety seat. He unclicked a few buckles, unsnapped a few snaps and lifted her out of the seat.

"Hey, sleepyhead."

She squinted, trying to open her eyes but not quite succeeding.

He laughed and grabbed the diaper bag.

Claire reached out to help him. "Let me take her."

"No. I've got her." He did. He had this baby who had been entrusted to his care. He'd never desert her. He'd do whatever needed to be done for her. He was officially a daddy.

As he walked down the plane's stairs, he noticed a big white SUV about thirty feet away. Leaning against the back door was his sister Charlotte. Tall and lanky, with shoulder-length brown hair, she didn't look one bit out of place wearing jeans and a Stetson…and were those cowboy boots?

He burst out laughing and nudged his head in her direction. "Would you believe that's my rebellious little sister Charlotte?"

Claire laughed.

Charlotte shoved away from the car and opened her arms to him as he approached. "What? You've never seen a cowboy hat?"

"I like your boots."

"Yeah, well, I like your baby." She took Bella from him and glanced at Claire. "I'm Charlotte, by the way. Matt's sister."

Claire reached out and shook the hand she extended. "I'm Claire. I'm helping him with Bella, the baby."

She peeked at Matt. "Where did you get a baby?"

He winced. "She's Ginny's little girl."

Her face softened. "Oh, Matt. I'm so sorry."

"So was I." Sadness rose up in him again, but only the sadness of a man who had lost a good friend, not the sadness of a man who had lost the love of his life. For the first time since he'd heard of Ginny's death, he felt at peace with it. "We're more concerned with getting Bella past it."

"Well, it looks like you're doing a good job." Charlotte bounced the baby playfully. "You're such a sweetie!"

Bella squealed happily.

Charlotte handed Bella to Matt, then opened the passenger door of the SUV with a wince. "Sorry. Since I didn't know you had a baby, I didn't bring a car seat. But it's a short ride. You can hold her."

"As long as it's a short ride."

"Very short."

Claire said, "Let me hold her in the back."

"That's probably a good idea." He handed the baby to Claire and stepped up into the SUV. Unexpectedly plush seats greeted him, but everything also seemed to have a longhorn motif. One of Matt's eyebrows rose.

Charlotte laughed. "Things are a little different here in Texas. Laid-back. Lucio had a bit of a time getting adjusted when we arrived, but he's fine now."

"Lucio? Your husband?"

"Love of my life."

"And where's Maria?" Matt asked, referring to her baby.

"She's back at the ranch, waiting to meet her uncle."

"So where's everybody else?"

She started the SUV and pulled away from the airstrip. "Everybody's at the ranch house." She peeked over at him. "Waiting to meet you."

A shiver of apprehension ran through him. It was the first time in his life he'd so desperately wanted something—not for himself—but for someone else. And he knew his past behavior might prevent him from getting it. That he'd disappoint and deprive Bella went through him like a knife.

Still, he ignored the fears rumbling through him. He wasn't just the Iceman on Wall Street. He'd survived getting a baby. Meeting a few half siblings would not throw him for a loop.

In only a few minutes, they were at the white clapboard ranch house. Simple and functional, it still somehow projected an air of stability and power. Corrals and outbuildings dotted the property. Horses grazed lazily behind the split-rail fence. Cattle roamed the pastures.

Everything was spit and polished, as if prepped for the big celebration the following week.

Wonder swept through him. An odd tingling. This is what he came from. These were his real roots.

After they exited the SUV, Charlotte took Bella from Matt and led him up the wood plank porch in back of the house. They entered through the door that led to a large kitchen. Men and women sat in the chairs around the cozy table. Others leaned against the cabinets. Matt's mouth fell at the sheer number of them.

His pretty blonde twin, Ellie, laughed, rose from the table and raced over. "It's so good to see you." She hugged him briefly and he closed his eyes as wave upon wave of emotion pummeled him. He didn't realize how much he'd missed his twin until this very second.

He had to clear his throat before he could say, "It's good to see you, too."

"And who's this?" Ellie said with a laugh as she reached for Bella.

Charlotte said, "Matt's baby." She pointed at Claire. "And that's Claire."

Everybody glanced at Matt expectantly.

He smiled. "Claire's helping me with Bella. Ginny and Oswald left custody of Bella to me."

A hush fell over the room, then everyone began to volunteer to help him with the baby. Bella was passed from hand to hand.

Charlotte continued with introductions. Ellie was with the town sheriff, Jed Jackson. Alex was there with a tall Australian named Jack. Megan Calhoun, one of Matt's half sisters, was "promised" to Adam somebody-or-another. There was a Nate and Sarah. A Jess and John. And Lucio holding Charlotte's new baby, Maria.

For the first time in his life, Matt wasn't afraid to take a newborn, examine her, pronounce her beautiful.

Everybody laughed.

Then a tall, dark-haired cowboy entered the kitchen. All talking stopped. A pretty blonde stepped up beside him, and Matt realized she hadn't been introduced when Charlotte was reciting couples.

Charlotte carefully said, "And that's Holt and Kathryn."

Matt's eyes met Holt's. The guy looked like he wrestled cattle for a living and given that he was the operator of this ranch Matt supposed he did.

"So you're the great Iceman."

CHAPTER TWELVE

LOOKING at Holt Calhoun, Matt swallowed. He had a choice. Assert his rights as oldest or simply say hello, extend his hand, create the bridge that would make all these people family.

He held out his hand.

"It's nice to meet you."

Holt stepped away from Kathryn. Took the hand Matt had extended. Shook once.

"Maybe we should reserve judgment on that." He pointed at the door. "How about a tour of the town?"

Matt glanced at Claire. She gave him a brief smile. They both knew this was Holt's way of getting Matt away for the discussion everybody knew they needed to have.

Yet it didn't feel right to leave Claire behind with so many strangers. "I'd love a tour of the town, if Claire and Bella can come."

"Oh, no!" Ellie said, taking Bella. "This little cutie stays. She's got cousins to meet and aunts to play with."

Holt glanced at Claire. "How about you, Claire? Do you want to stay?"

"Actually, I wouldn't mind a trip to town to get something a little lighter to wear." She tugged at the collar of her shirt. "It's hot down here."

Holt laughed. "Texas is probably hotter than Boston in October."

"So you guys go," Charlotte said. "We'll take care of Bella. Claire can shop for some cooler clothes." She smiled craftily. "And Holt can have his talk with Matt."

They piled into Holt's truck, which, luckily, had a back-seat for Claire. As much as she wanted some shorts and lightweight T-shirts, Charlotte's comment sort of frightened her about the upcoming conversation. She didn't really want to be part of a fight between the two oldest Calhoun sons…even if one was named Patterson.

She settled back on her seat as Holt said, "So what do you think?"

Matt said, "About what?"

Holt pointed out the windshield. "Everything you see is Calhoun land."

Claire couldn't stop her eyebrows from rising. That was a lot of land.

"I think our dad was a hell of an entrepreneur."

"And a good guy, too." Holt shifted on his seat. "At the banquet you'll hear stories of how he helped people." He glanced at Matt. "When I stepped into his shoes on the ranch the 'helping people' thing just sort of seemed to come with the territory."

Matt said nothing. Claire held her breath.

"I wanted to get you away from the rest of the family because I wanted to tell you that I recognize you are oldest. There's nothing in the will that gives me the ranch. Nothing that puts me in charge. I just did what needed to be done."

Matt glanced back at Claire and her heart stumbled in her chest. It was almost as if he was acknowledging her part in what he was about to say.

He looked at Holt again. "And you'll keep doing it.

I might be the oldest, but you're the best person to run things here in Texas." He grinned. "Now, if you'd like a little investment advice for profits and reserves, that might be something we could talk about."

Holt barked a laugh. And, to Claire's surprise, the conversation became cordial. Like a man proud of his heritage, Holt pointed out things of interest as they drove into town. Like a man curious about his heritage, Matt listened with rapt attention.

They passed Gracie May's Diner, the SmartMart, Gus's Fillin' Station and Hal's Drug and Photo store.

"The festival concerts will be held there," Holt said, pointing to a stage being built in what looked to be a park as he slid his truck into a space along Main Street. He jumped out and Matt took Claire's hand to help her out.

As he released her hand, she smiled at him and he returned her smile, as if he knew she would be proud of him. And by God, she was. This time last week, he would have grabbed his rights as oldest, just because they were his. After Bella—after *her*—he wanted to get along.

No. He wanted to do the right thing.

"Dad's banquet will be held in the Cattleman's Association Hall," Holt said when Claire and Matt rounded the truck and met him on the sidewalk. "I can show you that as we're driving home." He slapped Matt's back. "So while Claire's shopping, big brother, you have a choice. Coffee at Gracie's or a beer at the Saddle Up bar."

"Think I'll go for the beer." He faced Claire. "Will you be okay on your own?"

She grinned. After almost a week with Matt and Bella, it felt good to be on her own. "Yeah. I think I might explore a bit."

Holt laughed. "Not much to explore."

She chuckled and headed off in search of shorts and some tank tops.

An hour later, arms loaded with packages, not just clothes but souvenirs for Joni, she found the guys at Saddle Up, deep in conversation. As soon as they saw her, both rose. They were so different. Holt with his jeans and work shirt and a body built by hard work and Matt in his jeans and T-shirt and a whipcord lean, sexy body. Yet, they looked the same. It was clear they shared a bloodline. Even if Matt was better looking.

Of course, she was prejudiced. And happy. As if being in Texas brought out the best in him, Matt was chatty and solicitous. Immediately upon their return to the ranch house, he asked Kathryn which rooms they could use, saying he was sure Claire was eager to get into something cooler.

Because she was. As Holt had said, Texas heat was very different from Boston heat and she was drenched in sweat.

In the shower she tried not to make too much of Matt's behavior. But when she came downstairs, dressed in her shorts and tank top, and his eyes drank her in like a vintage wine, it was impossible not to notice that Happy Matt was here.

He sucked in a breath. "You look great."

She laughed. "It's only shorts and a T-shirt!"

"I know, but you have great legs. You should wear shorts all the time."

She laughed again. Not sure how to take his sudden, unexpected interest in her. She'd always known he was attracted to her. Hell, she was attracted to him. It seemed that in Texas he couldn't control it. Or maybe he couldn't control it because he was relaxed, happy. Letting himself do things he was too restrained to do in Boston.

"I don't think our climate would really support me wearing shorts all the time."

"Too bad." He caught her gaze. "Wanna check on Bella with me?"

"Yes, actually, I would."

They walked upstairs to the room where Bella and Izzy, Kathryn's daughter, had been sleeping, expecting to find two babies sitting up in the crib. But when they opened the door, they found four women, three babies—Bella, Izzy and Charlotte's baby, Maria—and Brady.

Walking into the fray, they began to separate. Matt took her hand. "We're looking for Bella."

Obviously having heard his voice, she squealed. Following the sound of the squeal, Claire found Bella sitting on Alex's lap. She walked over, taking Matt with her.

"How's our girl?" she said, then held back a gasp, realizing she'd more or less included herself into the group of Matt and Bella.

But Matt said, "Looks like our baby is fine."

Warmth filled her heart. He'd included her, too.

He let go of her hand and plucked Bella from Alex's lap. "What do you say, kid? Want some time outside with the old folks."

Bella squealed with delight. Not just because she wanted to go outside. From the way she reached for Claire, it was clear she was happy to see people she knew again.

Filled with love, Claire said, "Stay with your daddy."

Though Bella appeared a bit perturbed, she looked into Matt's face and cooed.

He laughed and carried Bella out of the room and downstairs, but everywhere they went a crowd of people had gathered. He caught Claire's hand again and led them outside.

She told herself it was nothing but a necessity, a way of

keeping them together. But she couldn't stop the hopeful swelling of her heart. What if having everything straightened out with his family had been the final piece of the puzzle he'd needed to be able to accept himself and move on. And what if she was part of that moving on?

After dinner—barbecue on a big outside grill, served on picnic tables with red-and-white-checkered tablecloths—the Calhouns and Pattersons talked about the ranch, their heritage and what they would be doing with the land, ranch profits and the other family holdings. Though half the people involved were neither Calhouns nor Pattersons, in-laws weren't just invited to sit in on the conversation, their opinions were respected and heard. Even Claire sat beside Matt, listening, participating when asked.

When the meeting was concluded, Ellie came over and sat on the bench seat next to Matt. She nudged her shoulder into his. "I have something to tell you."

"Me?"

"Yes. Jed and I are married."

"That's normally what people who are engaged do."

Claire stifled a laugh at his fun comment. Happy Matt, the man who loved to tease, was definitely here.

Ellie playfully punched his arm. "Be happy for me!"

He smiled warmly and little tingles danced up Claire's spine. She'd never seen him like this. Warm. Open.

Ellie grinned, then she drew in a slow breath, waiting for his answer.

In reply, he laughed—really laughed—and slid his arm around Claire's shoulders, as if drawing her into the intimate conversation. "I'm very happy for you."

Emotion flooded Claire.

Tears pricked at her eyelids. With Matt's arm around her shoulders and so much happy family stuff happening around her, she felt a part of things, too. And a rightness. As if this was exactly where she was supposed to be. That these people were her family, too.

Knowing that was dangerous thinking, she shifted to get out from under Matt's hold, but he held her fast, drawing her back when she would have moved away, as if silently telling her this was where she belonged.

Her chest tightened. She'd never felt so much love in a crowd of people before. Most of them might have only met this past year, but they were family. Solid. Dependable. There for one another.

And it seemed Matt wanted her to be part of that.

She couldn't even describe the emotions that bubbled up in her at that. After being alone most of her life, with a few friends and lots of scars from her failed relationship, she finally had a place where she belonged.

Around nine o'clock, everyone began to gather up their plates and serving dishes and head for home. Kathryn and Claire took the babies, Izzy and Bella, upstairs to bathe them. Holt left to go to the barn to talk with the ranch foreman. When the babies were in bed, Kathryn left to take a shower and Claire went in search of Matt.

Perfect peace settled over the ranch and caught Claire in its liquid warmth. With Matt behaving as if she belonged with him, it was hard not to spin fantasies. As much as she told herself not to, pictures of them together, forever, a part of this family easily formed.

She walked through the silent downstairs and found him on the front porch.

When he saw her, he rose from a wicker chair. "Want to go for a walk? Maybe see a little bit of the ranch?"

She glanced at him with a smile. "It's dark." And there weren't any streetlights as there were in Boston. Dark in Texas meant dark!

Matt shrugged. "Paths are lit."

She glanced over at the two paths. One led to a barn and was lit by light from the barn. The other led to the corral. That one was lit by light coming from the house. Still, it wasn't as if they had to worry about bumping into anything in the empty land. Plus, they hadn't had two minutes by themselves. With everything that was going on, he might have put his arm around her shoulders, held her hand and even included her in things with Bella, but he hadn't had a chance to tell her how he was feeling. The way he felt about her had changed—she could sense it in his touch—but she needed to hear.

"Sure. I'd love a walk."

They headed down the well-worn path. Claire looked up, amazed at the number of stars in the sky. "Look at all the stars."

"There's no city light blocking them out," Matt said as they walked down the trail. "What I can't get over is the quiet."

"Yeah." It was perfect. Everybody liked Matt. He liked them. And he liked her. Everyone had accepted her as if she fit, too. The peace of the ranch was like icing on a cake.

When Matt caught her hand, her heart swelled. This was it. She wasn't wrong. He liked her and she liked him. And though things weren't happening fast on this trip, she was glad. They'd connected so quickly in Boston that they could have made a mess of things. But here in Larkville, where time passed slowly and people moved slowly, they were regaining their equilibrium.

"Okay, so I was thinking," Matt said as he pulled her to a stop under a huge leafy tree. "I fit a little better than I'd imagined."

She laughed and stepped close to him. For once it felt right to act on what she was feeling. "You belong here."

"I think I do." He glanced around. "I also think I'm going to like being part of this family." He brought his gaze back to hers and smiled. "That's why I'm giving you your freedom."

She frowned. The words felt heavy, cold. Like stones that had been outside in winter. Out of place on this warm Texas night. "What?"

"Things fell into place perfectly here. And I have all kinds of sisterly help with Bella. It was an inconvenience for you to come here. So…" He smiled at her. "I'm letting you go home."

Her heart stopped as her brain tried to catch up with what was going on. "You're kicking me out?"

He laughed. "No. I'm letting you go home."

"But—" She stopped, unable to put what she was feeling into words. "You put your arm around me!"

Okay. That sounded stupid and maybe even childish, but it was the gist of what she felt. He'd made overtures all day. Done subtle, affectionate things. She'd thought they were connecting. For real. On a deep, intimate level.

She combed her fingers through her hair. She *hadn't* misinterpreted.

By the time she looked at him again, his eyes were narrowed, as if he'd been thinking through what she'd said about putting his arm around her. "You mean when Ellie told me she was married?"

"Yes." Oh, God. A horrible thought came to her. Had she misinterpreted his simple gestures because she liked him so much? Loved him, really. She'd been sitting on the edge of it for days and now she was here. Firmly in love with a guy who didn't want her.

Exactly what she'd promised Joni she would avoid.

She stepped back. "Okay. Yeah. You're right. I need to go home." She swallowed back a boatload of tears. Not just because she was losing something she really wanted, but also because she'd made a fool of herself. She didn't even have any pride left to save her. She turned and sprinted away.

"Claire! Claire, wait!"

But Holt picked that second to come out of the barn. "We have a bit of a problem."

Matt turned. "Problem?"

"I've got some numbers you need to see."

The "numbers" turned out to be the report of an investment that had gone south. The amount of money the family lost had been substantial, but a quick look at the rest of the portfolio put Matt's mind at ease. He explained to Holt that with a shift of a few investments they could make that money back and more.

He was glad he'd been able to help Holt, alleviate his concerns so he wouldn't have to go to sleep worried. But by the time they got back to the house, Kathryn was waiting for them in the kitchen.

"Did you tell Claire to go?"

Matt winced. This was the part of families that most men hated. Having to answer for things that should be private. Still, Kathryn was a wonderful woman. Someone Matt instinctively liked. He knew she wasn't prying, but concerned.

"I think Claire and I had a difference of opinion about her leaving. She's been helping me all week. I thought she'd be glad to go. But I think she wanted to stay. If she does, that's fine. She can stay. I'll talk to her in the morning."

"She's gone."

"What?" He shook his head. "She can't go. I didn't call the pilot."

"I think she flew commercial."

"Flew?"

"She was lucky to catch a flight that was leaving to-night." She frowned. "You do realize you've been in that barn for three hours."

"Oh." Matt sat.

Holt said, "Everything okay?"

He sucked in a breath. "Claire and I have sort of liked each other since we met at the adoption agency keeping Bella for me. I think her feelings went a little faster and a little further than mine." He smiled at Holt. "Her leaving is for the best. It would be a mess if she'd stayed. For both of us. But especially her. She needs to get back to work."

Holt nodded. "Okay, then."

But when Matt walked up the stairs to his bedroom and sank to his bed, alone, which he always was, his stom-ach flip-flopped. His feelings had been moving as fast as Claire's, and those gestures he'd been making all day—he hadn't been able to stop them. He liked her so much he couldn't stop touching her, wanting her. It was so easy to feel close to her, but he should have stopped his need to touch. Not just because he was afraid of something that happened so fast, but because she deserved better.

Much better. She might not realize it now, but his let-ting her leave was a gift to her.

CHAPTER THIRTEEN

MONDAY morning, Claire forced herself out of bed and into the shower. She washed her hair, put on makeup and slipped into her favorite red dress. Yes, Sunday had been a disaster of weeping and berating herself for falling for someone who didn't want her. But it was time to stop brooding over a man she'd known a week. She was stronger and smarter than that.

She knew Bella was safe and well cared for. She knew Matt didn't want her, hadn't seen her as anything but a helpmate. So feeling bad about it was only self-pity. And she didn't do self-pity. She picked herself up, dusted herself off and went on with life.

But even after that pep talk, by the time she got to the office, she was in tears.

Margaret, the receptionist, rose as Claire pushed open the Dysart Adoptions door. "Are you okay?"

"I'm fine," she said through a fresh round of sobbing.

Joni Dysart, the tall, thin blonde who owned Dysart Adoptions, came shuffling out. She put her arm around Claire, led her into her office and shut the door. "Oh, shoot. What happened to you going to Texas?"

"Oh, I went." She snatched a tissue from the box on the credenza, then fell to the seat in front of Joni's desk, as Joni sat on the tall-backed chair behind it. "And everything just kind of fell into place. With his family, he turned into the nice guy I'd been seeing glimpses of and suddenly he was doing things like holding my hand and putting his arm around me. I took it as a sign that we were feeling the same things." She peeked up and caught Joni's gaze. "But Saturday night, he told me I could go home."

"Simpleton!" Joni said with relish. "I could slap him! Don't pin this one on yourself. He doesn't want any woman. At least, not permanently." Joni handed the box of tissues from the credenza to Claire. "I told you he had a reputation."

"But we were different. We bonded over Bella."

Joni sighed. "What's the one thing we know better than anybody else?"

"That babies don't fix bad marriages or create relationships."

"Exactly."

"But he was just so different around her."

"Because he had a responsibility to be a good dad, and if there's one thing Iceman Patterson respects, it's responsibility."

"Oh, shoot. I know that. I always knew that. I just stopped reminding myself." Getting ahold of herself, she sniffed back the next round of tears. "What's wrong with me?"

"Nothing. You fell for a good-looking guy who was showing you his nice side because of the baby. And apparently the way he behaved with his family."

"Why didn't I see that?"

"Because you loved Bella. You wanted to see the best in him for her sake."

"I guess."

"Any woman would have fallen—"

"Being in love with someone after a few days isn't falling. It's leaping. I leaped into love with him—just as I did with Ben—except this time I knew it was wrong." She blew her nose. "I'm such an idiot."

"You're not an idiot."

"You're right. I'm not an idiot. So that only leaves desperate. His family made me feel so at home. A part of them. Like I finally belonged somewhere." She blew her nose again. "I'm a desperate woman who does stupid things."

Joni groaned. "You're not desperate, either. His family sounds very nice and he… Well, he's a great-looking guy. It would be hard not to be infatuated with him."

"And he truly loves Bella." She swallowed. "Okay. I get it. He was putting together a little family with Bella. And I…" She sighed. "I've always wanted a family. I guess it was hard to watch someone making one without trying to be involved."

"Look, I'm not the person to tell you your business, but maybe an actual vacation would be a good idea?"

"Vacation?"

"You were planning to take the week off, anyway. Why not go somewhere like a cruise…or maybe…Fiji…or Africa. Somewhere you'll be so busy you won't have time to think of Matt."

The thought of getting away for a few days lifted her spirits. "Maybe."

"Definitely. You fell too fast for the wrong guy. You need to clear your head."

Claire swallowed. Though she did agree she needed to clear her head, she didn't agree that Matt was the wrong guy. He might appear to be self-centered and cold to the rest of the world, but she'd met the real Matt Patterson. And he was wonderful. Everything she wanted. The problem was he didn't want her.

He might have been her right guy, but she hadn't been his right woman.

By Monday night, Matt thought his world had ended. No matter how many happy people were around him. No matter how many great things he saw, how many Larkville residents told him about his wonderful dad. No matter how much he loved seeing Bella with the other kids...

He missed Claire.

"You should just go and get her."

He faced Charlotte. "That transparent, huh?"

"Yes. We're all talking about it. We're just not doing it in front of you."

Normally, that would have made him mad. Knowing these woman usually talked out of love, not gossip, he laughed. "You don't understand. She's a wonderful woman. She deserves better than me."

Charlotte frowned. "Really?" She motioned for him to grab a bowl of macaroni salad and follow her out to the picnic tables they were setting for an impromptu supper. "It seems to me it's you she wants."

"And I'm not sure why."

"Seriously?" Charlotte laughed. "Could it be because you're handsome and smart and fun?"

"I'm not..." He almost said *fun*, then he remembered their water battle. He remembered laughing with her over Bella. He remembered teasing her and letting her tease him. He remembered putting his arm around her shoulders, as if bringing her into his family when Ellie told him she was married. Being with her made him fun.

They did love each other.

Charlotte stopped him halfway to the table, before they were in earshot of his other brothers and sisters and their mates. "Look, I don't want to be the one to tell you your business, but are you trying to repeat history?"

He gave her a puzzled look.

"Clay and Finella. Each lived without the love of his or her life. All because she wanted Clay to come after her and he didn't."

She paused, sucked in a breath. "Of course, we know now that he didn't get the letter she'd sent him, telling him she wanted another chance. But we also both know that though Mom was happy, there was always something missing from her life. Is that how you want to live?"

Matt looked away, thinking about his mother, knowing as Charlotte had said that there was always something missing from her life. Always a rim of sadness around an otherwise perfect existence.

"Clay didn't have a chance to get back the love of his life. But all you have to do is believe in yourself…believe in Claire…get in your plane and bring her back."

Standing in front of her closet, Claire whipped through the items hanging there, unable to find anything suitable for a vacation. Her clothes were old, and, worse, everything she owned was dowdy.

Was this how she'd seen herself in the years since Ben? Old? Uninteresting? Undesirable?

Tears filled her eyes. It was. She knew it was.

Until she met Matt. What she saw reflected in his eyes had made her feel like a woman again. A desirable woman. She'd been attracted to him because he was gorgeous. She'd begun to feel good about herself because it was clear he found her attractive. But she'd fallen in love because he was good, kind, bighearted, even if he didn't give himself credit for being any of those things.

She'd longed to be the person to show him how good he was, the same way he'd been the person to make her feel good about herself again.

But he didn't want that.

He didn't want her.

She whipped another shirt across the closet pole—a shirt she'd never worn because it was a dull, ugly purple. Why had she bought these things?

She finally found a sleeveless red top that might—and she stressed *might*—be okay for the flight down. But the sad truth was, she was probably going to have to buy a whole new wardrobe in St. Thomas.

She frowned. Would that be so bad? She had money. She needed clothes. She needed a whole new life.

Her doorbell rang. She tossed the red shirt to her bed and raced to answer, assuming it was Joni, here to make sure she didn't chicken out at the last minute and decide not to go.

Well, Joni didn't have to worry about that. Only a desperate woman fell in love in a few days…and with a man who kept telling her he didn't want her.

She *needed* a vacation!

As she reached the door, her heart protested. She didn't need a vacation. She needed love. She needed a man who challenged her and made her feel beautiful. A man who could be painfully honest. A man who understood her troubles because he'd lived something similar.

She needed Matt.

Telling herself she wasn't going to get him, she yanked open the door—

And there he stood.

Her mouth fell open. "Matt?"

"Hey." He shoved his hands into his jeans pockets. "Can I come in?"

Confused, she stepped back without thinking, motioning for him to enter. "I thought you were in Texas."

"I was. But after you left I realized I needed you."

He *needed* her? If it was possible for a heart to explode, hers definitely might.

With a shrug, he caught her gaze. "And Bella needs you."

Oh.

Her heart stuttered to a stop. She got it. He didn't need her the way she thought. He wanted a babysitter. Everybody he expected to be able to help him with Bella was probably busy with the festival or their own kids.

She held on to her poise by the merest thread. "You shouldn't have gone to Texas without hiring a nanny."

He chuckled—that wonderful chuckle that had taken him so long to let loose now seemed second nature, as if he was finally happy. Another arrow pierced her heart. He was happy without her. He needed a nanny, saw her as an employee.

"Bella needs more than a nanny. She needs you."

Drowning in the insult of him coming to her only for help with the baby and fearing she'd burst into tears, she turned away and headed for her bedroom, her head high, her shoulders back.

Insult and anger radiating through every muscle and bone in her body, she stiffly said, "I'm sorry but I'm booked on a flight to St. Thomas."

He scrambled after her. "St. Thomas? You're going on vacation?"

:"I don't see what business that is of yours."

"It's all kinds of business of mine!"

She whipped around. "Really? Why? Because you need a nanny and everything you want comes first?"

Hurt registered on his face first, then incredulity. As if he couldn't believe she'd said that. He took a step back, swiped his hand across his mouth. "Is that how you see me?"

Unexpected fear rippled through her. She didn't know what she was risking, but she suddenly knew if she answered his question wrong, she'd regret it for the rest of her life.

She blew her breath out on a long stream. Even forgetting the potential regret, her innate fairness wouldn't let her lay a guilt trip on him. He hadn't ever been anything but honest with her. He'd also warned her that if she got involved with him, she'd get hurt. They'd also only known each other a few days.

She had no right to be angry, or hurt, or even slightly insulted. She'd volunteered to help him.

"Okay, look. I had time to help you with Bella last week." She peeked up at him, then regretted it. His intense green eyes focused on her like two laser beams, reminding her of the day they'd met, when he'd truly needed her and she hadn't been able to resist coming to his aid.

She sucked in a breath. "But now I can't help you. I need a week away. A week for myself."

He tilted his head. "Why?"

"I'm tired?"

He laughed. "Yeah. Babies can be tiring. But you already had yesterday to rest. You should be fine... Why aren't you?"

Because you broke my heart?

Man, she wanted to say that! She wanted to say, "Look, you scoundrel. You broke my heart! And you can afford a nanny. So get lost."

But standing two feet away from him, so close she could touch him, something inside her shattered. He was the only person she'd ever really told about her dad. He was the only man who'd ever so honestly confided in her, trusted her with his most painful secrets. He was the first person she felt happy and beautiful with.

Her lips trembled.

"I didn't come here because I want you to be my nanny. I came here because I think I love you."

Her gaze flew to his.

"It's crazy. It's not wise. My sister told me that I should come here and ask you for a date, not ask you to marry me...but my gut says ask you to marry me."

She stared at him. "You're asking me to marry you?"

He nodded.

"Oh, my God."

"That's not a yes."

Unsure her legs could support her, she leaned against the wall.

He caught her by the elbows and pulled her to him. "It's crazy. It's weird. But I spent yesterday without you thinking I'd done the right thing because I didn't deserve you. Then I saw my brothers and sisters all happy and I thought, why not me? When Charlotte reminded me that my mom had left Clay Calhoun, the real love of her life and was never happy again, I knew I didn't want that to be me. When you're not with me, I feel like a part of me is missing."

She gazed up at him, whispered, "I've felt that, too."

"You don't have to marry me tomorrow. You don't

have to marry me next week or next month. We could still date."

She shook her head. "No." A laugh escaped. "Well, maybe for a while... Would you kiss me already?"

He yanked her to him and kissed her so fast, so powerfully, that her breath caught. His lips swooped over hers claiming her possessively, but she kissed him back, every bit as eager to seal this union and giddy with the knowledge that he loved her. This strong, smart, determined man had chosen her.

"What do you say we take this to the bedroom?"

She winced. "My bed's covered in clothes."

"Clothes?"

"I need new ones."

His eyes narrowed. "Now?"

She plucked at the front of his shirt. "Actually, I still have the clothes I bought in Texas and they'd be good for the festivities down there. But I need to buy something better for the banquet, if you're serious about marrying me."

He answered without hesitation. "You're the love of my life. I don't know how I know it, but what I feel for you is so strong I can't deny it."

"Then I think we'd better hit a store for a new banquet dress before we head back to Texas and Bella. I don't like both of us leaving her for too long. Besides—" She plucked at his shirt again. "I sort of thought we'd save making love."

He frowned. "Save it? Are you talking about waiting for marriage?"

She laughed. "No. But I would like to wait until we know it's right. Special."

He glanced around. "And taking you in your hallway wouldn't be special?"

She laughed again. "You can really be silly."

He grinned. "I know. I love it."

She rose to her tiptoes and brushed a kiss across his lips. "And I love you, too."

"So we wait?"

"Until we know that it's time."

"Honey. We have plenty of time. If I have anything to say about it, we have the rest of our lives."

EPILOGUE

COWBOY boots and tuxedos. If Matt had thought it strange to have the banquet in honor of Clay Calhoun in the wood-frame Cattleman's Association Hall, the cowboy boots and tuxedos topped that.

Prominent members of the community sat at the main banquet table, including Holt.

He resisted the urge to scowl at his brother. Holt had assumed that since he and Claire had returned to Texas "engaged," they were sleeping together so he'd put them in the same room.

Matt had secretly hoped that having only one bed would push the issue of making love, but Claire wanted their first time to be special, and for days he'd kept his promise. Luckily, going to the festival and getting to know his siblings had been so time-consuming that they'd fallen into bed exhausted.

They'd slept together but hadn't made love.

And that morning when he'd awakened beside her, he suddenly understood why she'd wanted to wait. With her hair spread out over her pillow and her prim pink paja-mas giving her skin a soft glow he realized how beauti-ful she was—how special. In all the hustle and bustle of realizing they were in love, then returning to Texas, and taking care of Bella, they'd never really had ten true romantic minutes.

But tonight he intended to rectify that. He'd bought a bottle of champagne, arranged to have their bedroom filled with roses and Kathryn had agreed to keep Bella with Izzy all night so he and Claire would have time alone.

He just had to get through this banquet.

One by one the speakers rose, talking about Clay Calhoun. His dad. His real dad.

Matt's chest tightened. His heart expanded. He didn't have to wonder who he was anymore, where he'd come from. He knew. The speakers told story after story of Clay Calhoun's kindness, generosity and love for the land.

He listened to stories of how his real father was a great man, and felt the seeds of that kind of strength living inside him.

Claire squeezed his hand. "You get that from him. The goodness you always tried to suppress. That's Clay Calhoun's impact on you." She smiled. "Good genes."

He laughed.

When Holt rose to speak, the entire room got quiet. He took the podium slowly, tapped on the mic, making it screech, and cleared his throat.

"My father," he said, "truly was a great man. Not because he did a few great things, but because he did a thousand small things greatly. He gave advice when needed, a helping hand when advice wasn't enough. I don't expect to fill his boots."

He met Matt's gaze from across the room. Matt nodded once, encouraging him to go on. He was proud of his brother. As proud as a man could be. And so happy to have finally found not just a family, but real love.

"So I can't fill his boots, but most of you know I'm there if you need me."

A general round of agreement rippled through the crowd.

"But the town's bigger than it used to be and one man probably couldn't help as many people as my dad could. Which is why we're glad there's a troop of us now. There are enough Calhouns and Pattersons that if one of us can't help you, another of us can. Just in case you don't know who we are, I'll introduce everybody."

He motioned to the long table filled with Calhouns and Pattersons. Family, Matt thought, once again overwhelmed by the importance of it.

"There's my sister Jess, her husband, Johnny, and their son, Brady." Tall, blonde Jessica and dark-haired Johnny rose, but adorable five-year-old Brady stole the show, waving to the crowd and causing a short burst of laughter to fill the room.

"Right beside them is Ellie Patterson, my half sister from Dad's first marriage and her husband, Jed. You'll know him better as Sheriff Jackson," he said, reminding everybody that Ellie's husband was the town sheriff. Holding Jed's hand, Matt's twin rose.

Something fierce began to build inside Matt. Pride and a connection so strong and so sweet it almost took his breath.

"Then there's Alex and Jack. They'll be back and forth from Australia, but they know they always have a home here." He motioned to the couple beyond Alex and Jack. "My sister Megan and her beau, Adam."

Because Holt was making introductions by going down the line of people sitting at the banquet table, Charlotte and Lucio, the next in line, rose automatically.

Holt smiled. "And that's Charlotte, her husband, Lucio, and their little girl, Maria." Charlotte fondly smiled down at Maria.

"After them, that's my brother Nate and you all already know Sarah." The couple rose and accepted a smattering of applause.

Then Holt stopped. He caught Matt's gaze again. Keeping with the spirit of the introductions, Matt took Claire's hand and stood.

Holt smiled stupidly. "And that guy who just rose? That's *my* big brother. Matt. Now most of you know, I like to be the one in charge but over the past few days I've learned my big brother knows a lot, and even though I'm the one in Texas, the one who will run the ranch and its holdings, Matt's the head of the family." He grinned again. "My big brother."

The crowd laughed. Matt shook his head and laughed, too. Claire squeezed his hand.

"If we can talk this guy into visiting Larkville a time or two every year, I have a feeling he could help us with everything from finances and start-up businesses to making hotcakes. His fiancée, Claire, happened to mention he's very good in the kitchen."

Everybody laughed again.

"Why don't you come up here and take your place, big brother? Say a few words."

Matt shook his head. He hadn't prepared anything to say. Wasn't sure what to say. Holt would still shoulder the burden of the family holdings. Matt was more or less a figurehead.

"Come on. Come up and say something. This is where you belong."

Where he belonged. It all suddenly clicked. This *was* where he belonged. It was where they all belonged.

Matt glanced at Claire. "Come with me."

She pressed her hand to her chest. "Me?"

"We're a team now."

She smiled and took the hand he extended. He led Claire to the podium, feeling odd, but also knowing that he'd come home. Maybe, just maybe, he really was supposed to head this family.

And when they got back to the ranch, he'd claim his woman, the love of his life, a woman he probably wouldn't have met if he'd been raised in Texas.

So maybe things did work out the way they were supposed to, after all?

* * * * *